Praise for Petra Hůlová

"Petra Hůlová is one of the most distinctive and outspoken Czech writers of her generation."
Project Plume

•

Praise for The Movement

"With echoes of *The Handmaid's Tale* but putting the women in charge, *The Movement* beckons us into a brave new world where men are institutionalized and re-educated—by any means necessary—to value women's inner worth. *The Movement* challenges and unsettles, offering a candid glimpse of the underbelly of feminist utopia, and raising important ethical questions about how far we might want or have to go in order to secure a truly equal world. Hůlová's distinctive voice is crystallized in Alex Zucker's fierce and flawless translation: this unapologetically provocative story is simultaneously a clarion call, a feminist manifesto, and a warning of the dangers lurking in both the old world and the new."
HELEN VASSALLO, *Translating Women*

"Hůlová's story can be read primarily as a timeless fable about how the best of human intentions always end up paving the road to some totalitarian hell."
Dublin Review of Books

"Petra Hůlová has managed to write a book that is committed in the best sense of the word: it unsettles, provokes, angers. It forces you to think while it also maintains a high literary standard."
MF DNES

"By setting her story in a dystopian world, Petra Hůlová has created room for a narrative that goes far beyond today's discussions in society about equal rights and protection for women."
Aktuálně.cz

"Petra is the first person I would give my pen to if she asked; Petra is a Pegasus, a creature of mythology; Petra has wings that let her fly above the people, cars, survey offices, social-welfare offices, beer tents, and double beds; she flies; then she types on her computer with her four hooves, pounding, beating, and asks herself: 'who are the people covering the sunlight?' Petra,

Pegasus, I throw my pencil up in the air for you; fly along; fly."

ARMIN PETRAS, director of *The Movement*'s German stage adaptation

•

Praise for All This Belongs to Me

"A beautifully fluent translation that portrays each character in convincingly idiomatic English, and yet still manages to distinguish the five closely related main characters according to their individual temperaments. The story is compelling on personal and broader, political levels, the characters are deeply human, and their difficult choices are portrayed with great dignity. All in all, this is a book to be savored and treasured."

JURY, American Literary Translators Association, National Translation Award

"An acutely observed account."
Times Literary Supplement

"*All This Belongs to Me* invites us into this singular universe created by Petra Hůlová, Mongolian but also abstract and timeless, and filled with memorable female characters that resonate with the readers."
World Literature Today

"A powerful story of roots and tradition, female strengths and weaknesses, personal tragedy and loss."
TripFiction

"What it led me into was a Mongolian urban society, in Ulaanbaatar, that I had not expected. Again, it was a breaking down of certain stereotypes as I read this book—our vision of Mongolia is the steppes and Genghis Khan, and that certainly is in the background, but the lives that these women are living are very much late-twentieth-century lives in a post-Soviet world."
Here & Now

•

Praise for Three Plastic Rooms

"An extraordinary and memorable read from beginning to end. A must for the personal reading lists for anyone who appreciates a unique and especially well-crafted novel."
Wisconsin Bookwatch

"The potential impact of *Three Plastic Rooms* on the Anglophone audience is greatly assisted by the experienced translator from Czech, Alex Zucker, who excelled himself at converting Hůlová's highly challenging colloquialisms into English without losing too much in the process."
EuropeNow

"*Three Plastic Rooms* is a journey through a person's soul in search of something resembling happiness and humanity in the gloating world of capitalism. A frighteningly honest novel—not easy to like, but impossible not to appreciate. The dark subject matter is somewhat balanced by Hůlová's verbal effervescence. She is a writer with a true passion for language."
Los Angeles Review of Books

"Taboo-breaking."
Asymptote Journal

"*Three Plastic Rooms* is unrelenting in both language and content, but beneath the sex scenes as foul as the language used to describe them it throbs with a rawness and a black humor that render this unlikely anti-heroine an addictive narrator."
HELEN VASSALLO, *Translating Women*

"A foul-mouthed Prague prostitute muses on her profession, aging and the nature of materialism. She explains her world view in the scripts and commentaries of her own reality TV series combining the mundane with fetishism, violence, wit, and an unvarnished mixture of vulgar and poetic language."
English PEN

"There is a build-up of intimacy amid the brutal and lyrical narration, attesting to Hůlová's generosity in this portrait, devoid of satire and facile judgement. A notable achievement."
Times Literary Supplement

The Movement

Petra Hůlová

The Movement

Translated from the Czech
by Alex Zucker

WORLD EDITIONS
New York, London, Amsterdam

Published in the USA in 2021 by World Editions LLC, New York
Published in the UK in 2021 by World Editions Ltd., London

World Editions
New York / London / Amsterdam
Stručné dějiny Hnutí
Copyright © Petra Hůlová, 2019
English translation copyright © Alex Zucker, 2021
Author portrait © Martin Rýz
Cover image © Cédric Roulliat

Printed by Zwaan Lenoir, Wormerveer, Netherlands

This book is a work of fiction. Any resemblance to actual persons, living or dead, or actual events is purely coincidental. The opinions expressed therein are those of the characters and should not be confused with those of the author.

British Library Cataloguing-in-Publication Data
A catalogue record for this book is available on request from the British Library.

ISBN 978-1-912987-24-5

First published as *Stručné dějiny Hnutí* in the Czech Republic in 2018 by Torst.

All rights reserved. No part of this publication may be reproduced, stored in or introduced into a retrieval system, or transmitted, in any form, or by any means (electronic, mechanical, photocopying, recording or otherwise) without the prior written permission of the publisher.

This publication has been supported by the Ministry of Culture of the Czech Republic

Twitter: @WorldEdBooks
Facebook: @WorldEditionsInternationalPublishing
Instagram: @WorldEdBooks
YouTube: World Editions
www.worldeditions.co.uk

Book Club Discussion Guides are available on our website.

She's really hit rock bottom, I thought. From the moment the elevator doors shut, I knew nothing was going to happen. I didn't even want to see her naked, I'd rather have avoided it, and yet it came to pass, and only confirmed what I'd already imagined. Her emotions may have been through the wringer, but her body had been damaged beyond repair. Her buttocks and breasts were no more than sacks of emaciated flesh, shrunken, flabby, and pendulous. She could no longer—she could never again—be considered an object of desire.

From *Submission* by Michel Houellebecq,
English translation by Lorin Stein
(Farrar, Straus and Giroux, 2015)

1

I had a suitcase, that's it. My mother's old suitcase with wheels, the one she used to take with her jetting around the Old World for work, till the doctor made her stop flying, because of her varicose veins.

It was late July, gruelingly hot, record-breaking temperatures. I forgot my bottle of water on the bus I took from where we lived to the town nearest the Institute. In our town, all we had was a recruitment office.

The woman there told me the Institute used to be a meatpacking plant and its current purpose was ongoing "small-scale" work. It had a capacity of such and such, its own brain trust, and, thanks to the generosity of its (all-female) donors, it could concentrate on its mission without having to compromise.

I already knew all that, of course, but the deciding factor for me was the availability of housing for out-of-town employees.

My mother was delighted when I gave her the news.

"Live your dream," she said. "And never back down from it," she added as I grabbed hold of that awful suitcase and walked out the door. It was a quote from a Movement campaign that no one remembers anymore, and even at the time my mother and I had found it a bit silly. Because you have to define what it means to not back down. Otherwise you risk sounding like some Nazi feminist offshoot slash self-appointed dictatorship of spoiled princesses, and nothing could have been further from the truth when it came to the Movement.

The clients' bedrooms are dark. Lights-out is at ten thirty, a policy the clients voted for themselves and submitted for approval, which the board rarely withholds. There's only one recent case I can think of, a seemingly mundane request to have mirrors installed at the Institute, to which the board replied as follows: "We mirror one another within ourselves. Not only women in men and vice versa, but also men within their own sex."

The request for mirrors was denied. The reason the board gave, in typical Old World fashion, was that it would overturn the fundamental idea of "Looking into the world and at it" in favor of "Looking at oneself with the intention of altering one's exterior to advertise oneself to others as an object for visual consumption, turning human beings into objects whose exterior is elevated at the expense of what lies within."

I remember the board's decision seemed a bit overzealous to me at the time, but I now understand and fully approve. The most unyielding walls of the Old World fortress are the walls within our minds. Although the Movement has been triumphant in most of its battles on the battlegrounds of the world (in our latitudes at least), the battles we fight with our own ways of thinking are waged behind the scenes, only after the curtain has come down.

The group of clients requesting mirrors

tried to counter with the feeble objection "We don't want to walk around the Institute with toothpaste on our faces," a weak lob the board returned with a smash, saying they could ask their roommates whether or not they had toothpaste on their face. And when one of the clients responded with the backhanded return "I don't have any friends here," the board put the point away with a brisk "Then ask the guards." Thinking back on it, I have to laugh, since in all my years here no one has ever asked if they have toothpaste on their face, and I always enjoy telling the story to novices at the Institute, as proof that it isn't only the clients who grow spiritually here, but also the staff, since at the time I had serious doubts about the wisdom of the board's decision.

If I had known that back then, on my grueling journey with that awful rattling suitcase, I could have spared myself a few lessons early in my employment, which I had imagined would be more like the work of a prison guard in Old World films, looking into cells through peepholes and that sort of thing.

Though, to be honest, that was so many

years ago now, I have only a vague recollection of what I imagined my work would be like, and my strong memories are all of how thirsty I was on the trip. The road leading to the Institute from the last stop on the city bus line was the kind that has a sign warning *ROAD CLOSED WHEN ICY*, but no gate blocking it off. That's how it was with everything in the Old World. Lies piled on lies piled on top of other lies, and ordinary human stupidity was just one more reason why the unethical environment for the upbringing of girls lasted as long as it did.

As we approached the Institute, I saw spots before my eyes and almost took the imposing building, divided into several wings and ringed with a thick wall, for a mirage. With all the cars coming and going and the road being practically dirt, I was covered in dust. It surprised me to see such brisk traffic, but the reason would have been obvious if I had stopped to think. How else were clients going to get to the Institute? The stop where I got off the bus was the end of the line, and not everyone could afford a taxi, which in any case was an option only for clients who lived in the next town over, and most of ours came from somewhere else. From places where there was no Institute. Either that or they had chosen ours because of its reputation, short waiting period (admission here, unlike at the smaller facilities, was almost always immediate), and outstanding results (the length of a stay was typically no longer than eighteen months). The Movement never bought into the idea of catchment areas. The freedom to decide one's place of treatment for oneself is one of the Movement's ethical maxims, and sometimes, too, the wives decide, based on a friend's recommendation or a visit in person (public days are the first and second Wednesday of every month). In fact, a woman who comes in advance to inspect the facility for herself is the best guarantee of a man's successful ongoing recovery at home.

Obviously, I knew none of this at the time. I attributed all the traffic to some bizarre detour, though I couldn't figure out why all the cars heading toward the Institute were driven by women, with the men in the back seat, most either asleep or in a daze. If anyone at the time had told me it was because the men were on pills, I probably would have been shocked. Even though it was generally known to be tough going with men before they entered the Institute. Especially if no one from their inner circle of friends had undergone treatment yet, they tended to have unfounded fears of retaliation. Manhood Watch was constantly trying to mislead men, claiming the only healthy choice was not to get any treatment at all, which was why we sent out patrol vans to pick up men and bring them to the Institute. The vans were the first thing I noticed, too, before the sheer size of the meatpacking plant took my breath away.

There are always patrol vans parked out in front of the plant, though the lot reserved for them is nowhere near as full now as it was when I started out, which makes sense, since the job of the patrols is to pick up men who are trying to avoid treatment and that number is steadily dropping. Voluntary admissions now exceed involuntary (what does victory look like if not this?), and the truth is many men look forward to coming to the

Institute, thinking it will give them a chance to relax. We're happy to let them believe that, though we're careful not to advertise our spa services. The main thing is not to lie, and our attorneys see to the rest. After all, what greater relief could there be than ridding your mind of stupidity—so when you get right down to it, a stay at the Institute actually is relaxing.

Most of the questions we get on open-door days have to do with our treatment procedures. I had the same questions running through my mind as I knocked on the reception desk window. In shifting gears from ideals to realization, things had broken down so many times before in human history that Manhood Watch would have been crazy not to use this fact against us, citing over and over the historic collapse of Communism, and every other -ism that they claimed lured people in with nice ideas, only to end in terror, chaos, a lower standard of living, and, ultimately, the corruption of the ideal itself, which, shorn of credibility, simply died away. The Movement viewed this scaremongering as a sign of success, since the acceptance of our beliefs as a "nice idea" was a monumental improvement over the days when we were labeled extremist, following the explosion in the Interior Ministry's basement—an act that catapulted the Movement, until that point seen as nothing more than a misfit collection of "unfucked women," into the public eye and gave Old World discourse the slap in the face that is now the subject of doctoral dissertations. Predictions of a debacle if our ideals were put into practice were clearly the tactic of a rear guard in retreat. The Movement was too strong to ignore. You can label a third of the population misfits but it's bound to backfire politically, and when a country erupts in protest, civil war is just one step away. Nobody wanted that. And maintaining the status quo by way of discursive dodges ultimately came to seem more complicated to anyone with any common sense than the "leap into the unknown" that Manhood Watch was warning against.

I was assigned an office, a housing unit, and a numerical code giving me access to spaces off-limits to clients and workers from other sections, except for section heads. I received a copy of the internal regulations and a set of work clothes. Then I was shown the cafeteria, the warehouses, a few of the client sleeping rooms, and even some of the clients themselves (men with normal responses and basket cases, too, no preselection by PR). To wrap things up, my section head devoted two whole hours of her precious time to me. Yes. The Movement values its workers and takes an individual approach to every client. We are all individuals and deserve to be treated as such.

"Stick to the discourse no matter what, as long as it doesn't come off flat. Otherwise it'll boomerang, take your head off like a slingshot. The trick is to use their strength against them," my first section head told me. Heavyset and in her fifties, she looked like the type of woman who ran a butcher shop, but in fact she held a long-distance degree from Oxford. Appearance is meaningless, as is hierarchy based on education and profession. My current section head actually did once work as a salesgirl in a butcher shop. One of the great draws for recruits to the Institute is the fact that there are no glass ceilings here, as I can confirm from my own experience. My tutor made herself available to me throughout my twelve weeks of training. I think of her often when I do the same for novices now, and more and more often nowadays some of them are men.

I'm sitting in a circle with my clients in Pavilion D, which falls within the scope of my duties and is under the direction of the Movement's regional branch. The view from my workroom is taken up by buildings that used to be part of the meatpacking plant before they were occupied by Idea and Work. The work of the Movement is to transform the Idea into Work, and as I tell the story of the little girl named Rita, some of the clients stare blankly out at the wall across the way, or through the windows giving onto the courtyard, which has been newly planted with decorative cherry trees (the bees' buzzing is so realistic, at first even I couldn't tell they were artificial, just like the cherries).

I usually start out: "Rita merely showed signs of heightened sensitivity to the injustices of the world around her." Then, to help the residents absorb what that means, I tell them about that world. About how little Rita and her mother were walking down a boulevard in the European metropolis where our story begins, and in typical Old World style it was lined with hideous billboards. Rita pointed to one and asked her mother the question that sooner or later occurred to every little Old World girl; and the reason an ethical environment for the upbringing of girls didn't exist in those days was precisely because the question wasn't raised. A question that should never have to occur to any little girl, not because they shouldn't think for themselves, but because there should be no reason for the question to occur to them—whether they formulate the question aloud, or keep it to themselves for fear of the answer and as a result it eats away at them, little by little, from the inside.

An ethical environment for the upbringing of girls means one in which they see themselves as a person who looks, not as a thing to be *looked at*. Little girls should be focused on looking out at the world, not on how somebody else looks at them, or on outward appearances, the way their mothers often were, worrying if they looked sexy enough. And little girls in the Old World would stare in astonishment until they got used to it, until they got over the horror of being their gender, which is what's known as accepting things for what they are for your own good. Paving the way to your own hell for your own good, to put it in terms that everyone can easily understand.

People used to say (out of earshot, of course): Your value as a person drops by one point every hour after the age of twenty. But you don't find out what your total allotment of points is until the gong sounds, announcing, "Deduct for face and figure," meaning your femininity index has declined to near zero (pharmaceutical firms were clearing record profits from the sale of estrogen pills when the Movement chalked up its first modest successes). In the Old World, even women with fairly ugly faces could usually still make the grade by squeezing their bodies into shorts reinforced with a triple layer of Lycra, since no one much cared about faces anyway, and though a few studies in the pre-Movement period looked at what happened to women who lost their femininity, no one could define femininity without reference to charm, and any definition of charm broke down the moment youth was out of the picture. A few women, undeterred, declared that they still *felt* young, and there was some media propaganda to back them up on this (depressed women are less productive at work). Plastic surgeons and the cosmetics industry, however, promoted the thesis that "feeling isn't enough," arguing that a woman's age should be concealed as much as possible, not only because a penis would fail to sustain an erection in the presence of an openly geriatric vagina, but because the whole thing was so inextricably tangled up with love.

In short, the times were not merely ripe for change, but desperately crying out for it. Still, some claimed it was a hormonal deviation caused by pollution. They said sex drives in older women were no longer as strong as they used to be (although, according to Movement ideologues, the sex drive of older women "just wasn't discussed in the past"). In the Old World, women were supposed to renounce desire once they reached a certain age. Making an effort to be attractive was viewed as a silly bother, though deceiving people with your looks was viewed as acceptable, since it was a way for women to ensure their right to love. It's true. That's how desperate things were in those days.

We had to scramble to get our bearings in the new reality, after thousands of years of "not giving a shit," and yes, being criticized for being vulgar, too. I say "we" because I subscribe to the Idea. Back then I was a little girl.

My feelings as a child were similar to the way I felt driving in the car with my mother, cluelessly winding down one poorly paved district road after another, trying to find the village where we could turn onto the main road. My mother always drove with the GPS off, to toughen herself up, as she put it, for the moment when the hackers would bring the world's machines to their knees. As she sat behind the wheel swearing at the dark and rainy weather, I enjoyed the adventure, but still I was scared.

I tell my clients: "The question Rita posed

to her mother, pointing to the billboard as they walked along the street, was: 'Mommy, why is that lady naked?'"

Whether the pair of full-figured breasts in a micro bra and the butt cheeks hanging out of high-cut shorts were an advertisement for peanuts, herb butter, paint supplies, or the latest pulse-tracking device has long since been forgotten, but Rita's question has become a milestone. In fact Rita herself later referred to it as the origin of the awakening that led to the Movement's founding. An awakening from eons of humiliating limbo. The symbolic start of the revolution.

There are those who claim that Rita's story has been falsely embellished by supporters of the Movement. That her life is wrapped in an aura of lies. That the fate of the founder's mother is fabricated, distorted, and at least half-invented, so as to manipulate, glorify, and explain a societal sea change that makes no sense to them. In short, it doesn't suit their plans. Rather than offer a counterargument, I will simply say this: The story I'm telling here is the one I have available. I am not overstating, misrepresenting, or inventing the things I have heard, read, and experienced, and if anything I say here took place any differently from how I describe it, it does nothing to change the fact of where we ended up.

"My mother's silence was ominous," Rita would say with a smile whenever she told her story at Movement gatherings. It was a smile that appeared in countless photographs and TV broadcasts, and, once the Movement became more established, at prestigious universities whose honorary doctorates Rita declined with the same smile every time. Her existential orientation ruled out any collaboration with these institutions, which, despite the intellectual resources at their disposal, in all their years of operation still hadn't been able to achieve what Rita had. A girl from an ordinary family who started out with nothing, she dragged the truth into the light like a mirror in which the Old World couldn't help but see itself for what it really was, and only then did it begin to rise up and fight back. In the Old World, women's half-naked bodies were put on display to be ogled by random passersby, serving no purpose other than commerce, the sale of goods. Not only was no one held accountable for this unethical environment, but hardly anyone gave it a second thought. So the Movement was left with no choice.

My office is no different than anyone else's. They give guards the same offices as they do administrative and therapeutic staff. I don't try to hide the fact that it's only on loan to me with any framed family photographs or cushions casually tossed on the couch. I'm at work, and to pretend it's anything else wouldn't be fair to the work. Work wants to be work. Which doesn't in any way diminish its meaningfulness, or my zeal for it.

Superficial treatment isn't worth shit, the section head says whenever she has a bit too much to drink at parties, and yes, we have parties here like any other workplace: whenever someone has a birthday, moves to another department, or retires. A cosmetic change in personality, "being on one's best behavior," is pointless. Anything other than a deep personality change isn't enough to be cured, and cruel though it may be, it needs to be said, for the sake of full disclosure, that we remove a part of our clients' interior. In short, we seek to excise a portion of their inner selves, and yes, we are doing so in hundreds of concurrently running workshops as we speak. The only theoretical disputes concern whether or not it's necessary to implant something else in place of the excised part, or whether it's enough simply to rid the client of the "cancerous tissue" and let the organism heal on its own. Passionate debates among Institute workers on all sorts of topics often extend into the early hours of the morning, in the conference hall on the ground floor of Pavilion c (the former slaughterhouse), or in more intimate conversations among clusters of workers outside our offices. But they're basically arguments over details. Because all of us are united by the Idea, and I don't mention these discrepancies as proof of discord in our ranks but as proof that anyone can say anything they want, because even today you still encounter the retrograde view that the Movement's praxis and ideals are totalitarian.

Work for the Institute is voluntary, and

so are stays, with some exceptions. These exceptions, however, prove the rule, which is to reject the idea that a woman's exterior is more important than what goes on inside her and that this outward appearance should be viewed through the lens of a femininity defined as sex appeal based on youth. So it's actually more a creed than a rule, and the number of exceptions proving this rule will soon be zero. The word that comes to mind in this context is *originality*, and if this were a drama, which is what some of my colleagues use to teach our clients, I would say "it brought tears to their eyes," since the Movement's beginnings are inextricably linked to the originality of the Idea, and even though our originality was criticized, in reality the most original thing about the Movement is the determination to see our ideals through to the end, which for that matter could have and should have been done ages ago.

The Old World loved the word *originality*. It was obsessed with it. The type of originality that dressed the woman on the billboard—the one Rita saw with her mother when Rita was a little girl—in a swimsuit striped white, blue, and red, the colors of the national flag, instead of one with sparkles. It was even described as a matter of patriotism. Yes, Manhood Watch used anything they could get their hands on, even Czech nationalism—whatever it took to help them "get through to the people" so they could talk them out of the Movement's ideas.

The office windows are sealed airtight, since the Institute circulates its own climatized air, cooled or warmed depending on the needs of workers and clients, as well as for safety reasons. Years ago, I was told, one of my colleagues had a child fall out the window—they pushed a chair to the window while the guard wasn't watching. Evil tongues later claimed several workers refused to offer the woman condolences, since the child was a boy. Clearly a slander on the part of Manhood Watch, since I've never encountered a colleague that inhuman in all my time here. Others claim the Institute has always had the windows sealed shut, because of the smell left over from the days when it was still a meatpacking plant. Whatever the case, I managed to pry mine open, so now I can open or close it as I please, and if I lean out far enough, even the smoke alarm can't tell. Sometimes, when I feel ridiculous about all the hours I've spent leaning out the window, I'm tempted to try lighting up right at my desk to test my suspicion that the alarm in my office is fake. Yes. I am a compulsive smoker and engage in the habit even while reading letters. We monitor clients' correspondence for their own good, just like yours is monitored for my good, and mine for yours. We got used to it a long time ago. There's nothing to hide.

The letter I have in front of me right now is from a few days ago and opens with the words *Dear Mom*, which caught my attention since most of our male clients' letters are addressed to their female partners, who occasionally sign out the men against our advice, at the clients' instigation of course. Widowers (we take special care of the bereaved of women who fall victim to police brutality during one of our demonstrations) and older single men usually write their mothers, and their letters, almost without exception, testify to their process of self-reflection. Phrases such as *I never suspected that* or *How come you never told me about* or *If only I had known, I would have* raise the senders' ratings, signaling the awakening we're looking for. We state this not only in our informational materials, but also directly to the clients, as follows: Punishment is reserved solely for deliberate sabotage of medical procedures or violation of the rules. One of the most common violations is the consumption of pornography, which to a great extent was eliminated by cutting off the internet, so that now the web is accessible only to our workers, and it's also up to them to track down what remains: printed pornographic materials stashed away in clothes, under mattresses, in bedding. Reports by fellow clients also help with that.

I reach for my lighter. The letter from client number three-forty-five ends with the words: *His whole life he cheated on you, and yet you stayed with him. How come?* It's these last words that really get to me, the beginning and end of so many horrors, the prolapse of Old World morals. "Take your suffrage and shove it" was one of the Movement's first slogans, written by a woman of retirement age—later a close associate of Rita's—in paint on a bedsheet, which she then wrapped around herself and wore, like a senator of the Roman Empire in decline, walking around her hometown for a week. Gradually, other women joined in. When we teach the history of the Movement at the Institute, we don't mention this other woman, but only to avoid overwhelming the clients with names. So, in short, Rita was the detonator, but she couldn't have done it on her own, and not only for logistical reasons. (This was also why she so stubbornly refused to accept doctorates and rejected the idea that some Institutes should bear her name.) The reality is, there were soccer stadiums full of people who carried the torch with her.

Your beloved Libor ends the letter from a client in my group in the corner block on the third floor of Pavilion B. Libor ran a branch of a small bank, and though in his free time he devoted himself to refurbishing printed circuit boards, when it came to the technological imitation of womanhood—the product of deranged brains resulting in custom-made (aka "privately modulated") porn: animatronic fucking torsos, remote-control vaginal sleeves, and whole armies of sex dolls whose preset conversations, despite the best efforts of the so-called designers in the days of Libor's youth, barely reached the intelligence level of a household pet (they could bring your slippers but couldn't catch a mouse)—all he had to say, in an exchange with his therapist that I found in his file, was, "I never gave it any thought," and that's true of most clients. They aren't guilty, they only feel that they are. The evil of the Old World was its inability to think things through to their consequences, while technology was thinking things through to the tiniest detail (although solely from the standpoint of user experience), which means it not only didn't care about the exchange rate, but it also didn't care what currency was used. And Libor's sign-off has me itching to lower his rating (a single click is all it takes), because instead of ending his letter with love for his mother, he declares her love for him.

I close Libor's folder with a footnote, password-protect the file (yes, we get hacker attacks here, too), and stub out my cigarette in the mug containing what's left of my ion drink. Overtime is what keeps the Institute running smoothly. We're paid a salary, rather than an hourly wage, and even though it says so in our contracts (the realization of ideals involves paperwork, which qualifies as a success, not a drag, since it means the Movement's ideals are a part of everyday life), even though it says so right there, in black and white, some of my colleagues still complain about the workload, and that's mainly because the Institute suffers from a chronic shortage of workers. And in case I failed to mention it yet, yes, men work here too.

If I lean out the window with a cigarette and I'm not in the middle of an especially impressive client letter, it usually means I've clocked out for the day and I'm just blankly staring at Pavilion F across the way. That's the one where they processed scrap when this was a meatpacking plant (the last remaining cattle were, for ethical reasons, slaughtered back when I was still in school), later converted by the Movement into the clients' quarters.

With the sun screened out by the overhanging roof, residents are prohibited from having curtains in their windows, which allows us to monitor their activities from our offices during our time off. There are cameras installed in the sleeping rooms, though the signal drops out every now and then.

However hard the Manhood Watch hackers try to paralyze the Institute, the main result when our network goes down is violent attacks with a homoerotic subtext among the clients themselves. Plus, now, not only can they wave to us on camera (in which case the technician on duty is responsible for making immediate contact via the two-way speaker located in the corner of their room), but they can also signal us directly through the windows.

Most clients wave at the window of the section head overseeing their progress, or at their guard, who has the most contact with them. Which means employees don't have curtains or blinds on their windows either. And to illustrate to clients just how much the Institute prioritizes them, I point out that the roof with the overhang to block out the sun (for the past decade, hot summers with temperatures averaging over ninety degrees have been the rule) is only on their quarters; the buildings where our offices are don't have that roof.

The Institute puts most of its funds toward researching treatment methods and raising the housing standard (our image as spartan took a long time to shed; the conversion of the meatpacking plant was a hectic process and during the trial period the building lacked not only elevators but also enough pillows). Investing in a comfortable work environment is of secondary priority, and often doesn't happen at all, which proves that the Institute values its clients. This is something we can afford because while we're driven by an idea (it isn't the low pay that drives us), the clients are supposed to be getting rid of most of theirs, and none of the employees would dare deny that the process is painful and difficult, or that having good conditions is more important for the work of the clients than it is for ours, our work being merely that of guides and coaches.

I stub out my third and last cigarette of the day on the windowsill and peer out the window into my clients' quarters. With the rays of the sun, all I can see are their silhouettes, and, almost as if they can tell, disputes tend to occur around twilight and the cameras seem to drop out to spite me; clients can recognize this by the fact that the green light next to the lens goes dim. Then the following day, in morning circle, they report a stolen watch, a kick in the groin, a deliberately spilled-on bed, and our informants report the consumption of porn by their incorrigible colleagues.

I'm here because of my ideas and also because I felt the need to be independent. To move away. Not to get away from my husband, like the women who set up communes (not just in the villages, where they lived off of produce and homemade cheeses, but also in towns and cities, where all the banks with majority-women boards merged), but to get away from my mother. My mother was a typical case of someone in the gray zone of tacit agreement with the Movement. Her support consisted of subscribing to the e-zine, which carried all the latest information on the Movement, and setting up a regular donation that went direct from her bank account to the Movement every month. This was typical of the Movement's improvised beginnings and was only later recognized for the brilliant strategy it was. The extensive matrix of women who subscribed to the e-zine—a matrix of women absolutely indistinguishable on the street, unlike the zealous young women of the old days who showed up with baby carriages and buttons on their backpacks to demonstrate for marginal movements opposed to the construction of highways or to reductions in cultural subsidies—was also a subject of discussion in the Movement's free public courses (which were more about boosting women's courage than conveying information).

The women in the gray zone of tacit agreement, which included my mother, were designated "agents," because even the secret services didn't uncover most of them, and because of the memorable declaration of the then Minister of the Interior, who stated, "We are on to the core of this extremist organization" at the very moment that Rita and her inner circle, disguised as electric-meter readers, were in the basement of the Interior Ministry, installing their first explosive device.

I didn't make a peep when my mother told me these things. Including about the bank account, which they seized just before the Movement's designation as "extremist" was withdrawn, since you can hardly consider a solid third of the nation to be extreme. In retrospect, the Movement's achievements seem to have come remarkably quickly, but the women who lived through them claimed that between the start of the protests and their massification there were moments when it looked like "they would pick us off one by one and lock us all up," or that "Manhood Watch would string us up from the lampposts as a warning, like they did to the Communists during the uprising in Hungary."

I held my breath when my mother told me that story; I would have given anything to have been there to see it. Nowadays the arbitrary treatment of a woman, the degradation of a human being to the status of object for the purpose of selling something, by exploitation of the basest pseudo-evolutionary mechanisms, will land you in jail, and the fact that nobody is sentenced for those things anymore isn't because, as in the Old World (typical of a society where exterior is elevated over substance), the perpetrators have excellent lawyers, but because nobody would dare do those things. This is the Movement's true victory, and in corporate jargon they call it restructuring (though in our case we're getting rid of prejudices, not people)—and I should add, for the benefit of any primitive thinkers reading these memoirs, that thanks to the abolition of billboards featuring half-naked women, there was also a drop in traffic accidents.

Registration for clients is similar to the onboarding process I myself went through. They're introduced in the same way and take the same circular route around the Institute, except that, obviously, clients aren't given the numerical code that grants me access to areas where they aren't allowed.

As far as internal regulations go, there are only minor differences between the clients' privileges and mine (they can smoke around the communal ashtray in the yard, but not in the kitchen), and more of their tour takes place in the garden than the one for novices, again for obvious reasons: apart from the Institute interior, it's the only area clients have access to throughout their stay (with access limited only in connection with certain punishments: Internal Regulations, chapter four, article five).

Throughout the admission process and tour, clients are typically accompanied by their partners, who in most cases have already visited during open-door days, so they can offer psychological support, and women often support their male partners physically as well, especially when the men's legs start to shake. The most common questions, apart from medical procedures, concern meals, lights-out, the daily regime (to the frequent question of whether there are morning calisthenics, we repeat: No, and not at night, either), and staying hydrated: where to go when the canteen is closed, since the water in the toilets isn't potable (one of the most on-point jokes about the Old World is that they even flushed with drinking water). The answer: to the tea urn in the hallway, or ask a guard and she'll get you a drink from the kitchen. Then they want to know how long the man will have to stay, which of course is solely up to him, but there are those who think we can determine that in advance based on the intake interview, in which case our workers are quick to disabuse them of this belief.

We don't pull the wool over anyone's eyes. When I first started, the Institute used to give an estimate of the time required for treatment. We stopped doing this because the human mind is inscrutable, which is the beauty of it, and besides, we don't want to give our clients any false hopes.

Which brings me to something fundamental, and that is optimism. Optimism in the approach to treatment, throughout the reeducation process, and even in those moments when the treatment has fallen short and a section head rejects a client's request to take the final exam. Yes, optimism is impossible to maintain without support, but the Movement knows that, which is why the Institute offers such a rich variety of programs: art therapy, gastrotherapy (amateur culinary school), hypnotherapy, aromatherapy, etc. Optimism also means that, as a client, I believe in my reeducation, despite that "When I look at a woman, I still see mostly ass—tits and ass. Even after three months' treatment, I couldn't care less about her inner complexity as a person." MK, such and such a date, such and such a year, Pavilion D, Bedroom 158.

I'm sitting in my office, going over text again. This time, it isn't letters to women from clients, but self-criticism, which the clients submit at the end of each duly completed course. Every client has to go through the workshop, which is the pillar of our reeducation, preparing clients for the final exam, but hypnotherapy, for example, is voluntary, and there are sliding time slots for the courses, so not every client has their final exam on the same date. Schedules are individual, clients onboard on an ongoing basis, so we don't have a start of semester or end of school year.

Mornings, I greet the clients as I hurry down the hall to my office, smiling at the ones who are mine; some are on their way to cook French onion soup, others have horse grooming to look forward to, and some, pale and shaky, are heading to the assembly hall for their final exam (which we hold, depending on the number of clients, a maximum of two or three times per year). Assuming they pass the exam, they pack up their things that same day and set out into their new life.

"I request transfer to a section with a male instructor," MK writes in his self-criticism. At the end of a demanding day, I'm relaxing in the window with a cigarette and thinking I'll have to pay him a personal visit as soon as possible.

"When the instructor lectures us on New World ethics, all I can think about is her cunt, imagining against my will what it would be like for us to have sex. This is even though I've abstained from porn since entering the Institute and taken part in every procedure without a single absence," he writes.

Confessions like this are a daily occurrence. They demonstrate: 1) trust in the Institute's treatment and workers; 2) the doubts that inevitably accompany treatment (time and again, we urge clients to be patient, emphasizing that adaptation alone can sometimes take as long as six months); and 3) a willingness to work on oneself. Just the opposite are the confessions laden with criticism (of the Institute, the Movement, and the New World in general), complaints dripping with self-pity (lowers their rating several points), or lengthy essays demanding porn, a lower dose of medicine, or a night with a novice. This last tends to happen when clients mistakenly interpret a novice's generous offer to be available "any time for anything" as an Old World proposition, imagining her "anything" as a reward for what they call "exemplary results in their coursework." Which means they'll have to complete their courses again with increased supervision and this time pay attention during class.

I stub my cigarette out on the windowsill, watching as a group of clients in a corner of the courtyard ride horses under the supervision of an instructor. Horseback riding is of course only partial compensation for the lack of intimacy and physical contact that clients suffer in the early days of their treatment. But even that is part of the order of things. And their celibacy doesn't serve some screwed-up idea of purity (the false Christian concept that a woman's body is filthy), but as space for the kinds of emotions and thoughts that don't crop up except in a state of mental emptiness.

"Sometimes I don't understand what's expected of me," writes OP. And as for the "human factor," let me briefly say this: it's everywhere, at all times. The Institute is neither "inhumane" nor "dehumanizing," as Manhood Watch have tried to claim in countries where the Movement has yet to establish a presence (they're organizing a tour of those countries under the name Prevention of the Age of Decline, funded by chauvinist donors), and as I'm reflecting it dawns on me: it isn't actually him, but OP reminds me of Ondřej Pěkný, an elementary school classmate of mine with horrendous politics.

It may sound cruel, but these kinds of encounters with the Old World, in the form of men we know who suddenly turn up as clients, evoke strong emotions when my colleagues and I meet in the kitchen over coffee. Some of my colleagues ridicule them and make inappropriate comments, but the truth is, more often than not, they're simply deeply moved.

In our promotional materials, available along with buttons, T-shirts, mugs, and sweatshirts in the gift shop on the ground floor to the left of the main entrance (on the right, past the fountain, which gives a first impression of the Institute as more like a spa than it deserves), there are several references to the Institute as "family." This is a bit of a stretch, of course. When I came on staff, my section head told me, "Whatever you want to know, ask me. The promo materials in the gift shop are mainly for the wives that come on open-door days." For simple women whose trust needs to be gained in a simple way, because they're about to make a life decision, and what they need is support and the feeling they're understood, rather than a laundry list of information. They'll get plenty of that when they return with their husbands, and even though they can back out at any point (until after registration, when we get their signatures), a woman who comes to the Institute with a man only rarely goes back home with him, under circumstances that can typically be prevented through the use of medications also mentioned in our portfolio. And although the men usually nap in the back seat while the women drive their cars down the dusty road that leads here, even on medication they're still capable of driving, and can perform their jobs with no limitations right up until the day they're admitted.

"What is expected of you is to submit to the educational program without exception," I tell OP straight up and truthfully, in response to his question of what the Institute expects of him. The point of answering the questions clients formulate in their self-criticisms is not to put them in their place but to give them direction, not to cut them off but to give them a nudge. We may engage in debate over the optimal balance of treatment, but there is unity on the point that both medication and electroshock therapy (precisely targeting specific areas of the brain) are merely supportive. The main thing is self-reflection, practice, and above all, the will to work on oneself. And even though ultimately OP must fully and completely surrender to the educational program (as he knows very well, given how many times it's been driven home), what he's really asking is why he should do it. It takes me just two clicks in his personal file to learn he was brought here by one of our ambulatory vans, but his question alone speaks for itself and demonstrates this much: he didn't receive the appropriate ideological processing before entering the Institute. It may sound awful, but it's clear. Only our own intellectual labor can prepare us for transformation. Without that, we can't understand the point, we lack the willingness, and when effort is required (the superhuman commitment of our clients), frustration, understandably, changes to resistance.

During my first few days at the Institute, I asked under what circumstances we could use the electric baton, and my section head got pissed. "If it's demanding, they don't want to do it, and they also won't do things without a clear reason," she said sourly. Rita wrote: "Violence is reserved for extreme circumstances."

We expect our clients to have empathy for women and we have the same duty toward them. "It isn't his fault he wasn't adequately prepared by either his wife or society," I drone to myself about a client as I fill in a form requesting a leave of absence from work. Everyone here battles burnout from time to time, and we're encouraged not to be ashamed of it. Better a business trip or a vacation than to have a worker collapse (it's happened twice right in front of me) or submit her resignation when it could have been avoided.

"Visit me next week during consultation hours," I tell OP, and even though he must have at least some idea why he's here and what's expected of him (our ambulances are only authorized to bring men here in clear cases), I add: "It's for your own good," only then going into the details. "It's about a certain way of seeing things," I say. "You avoid electroshock treatment by volunteering for it," and in the course of my consultation with him I pull a folder out of my bag containing photos of women's genitals.

Although some of my colleagues include all the alleged "juicy details" and the "defamation by Manhood Watch" when they tell clients the history of the Movement—Rita never learned how to read; she would secretly dress up as a man; she was paranoid; she didn't speak until she was eight years old; she suffered from cirrhosis of the liver in old age due to alcoholism—personally I stick only to facts and verified information.

"Unfucked cunts," they called members of the Movement in the days before it established itself. They also used to say Rita had fat calves and a stubby neck, and that as a child she was abused by either her stepfather or her volleyball coach. The false prophets of Manhood Watch recommended psychotherapy, saying, "The woman needs to be institutionalized." They claimed they "feared for her sanity." "Hospitalization, the easy way or the hard way." Most of them were men who ended up in Institutes themselves, and some are among those committed for lifelong reeducation, a fact I keep from the clients for now, since they're still new and I don't want to scare them.

For me the history of the Movement is only those parts that carry the torch, the sequence of social actions that illustrate changes in its "vision." The rest is just the mechanism by which those changes were introduced into daily life, and the "juicy details" are nothing but short-lived gossip. The only reason they hold any interest is because to explain the Movement's phenomenal success as the result of its ideological power alone is "sometimes beyond their capacity to imagine," one of my colleagues says of the clients who cling to conspiracy theories—and also sometimes clients drift off during seminars, so my colleagues try to wake them up with this cheap gossip. Horse crap. Through the tangles of smoke from our shared cigarette in the kitchen, I listen to my colleague's stories about the clients she questioned last week. She was tasked with updating the list of their ideas and requests. They said they wanted a ping-pong table, more frequent changes in the type of tofu in the dining hall, longer outdoor breaks, better gardening tools (the special zone for floriculture is an initiative of our section that we started about a year ago, I brag to my colleague), and alcohol at least once a month. The last request could only mean the client was just having a laugh at her expense, since they all know chapter one of the rules by heart.

Just as I couldn't care less about Rita's private life, I keep my colleagues' interest in mine within limits. Using a person's private life to explain their career motivations is a bad habit that unfortunately some of the younger staff—the ones who see their work at the Institute as a "solution" to their personal problems, a sure sign of immaturity—haven't gotten over yet, and the caliber of their work generally isn't too high either.

"I'm halfway through life, and when I imagine everything that still needs to be done in that last third, when your energy is dwindling, it seems impossible unless you give up on having a personal life," my section head said recently. Like me, she worked her way up from nothing, and unlike some of my stuck-up colleagues from so-called better families, she doesn't wield her job at the

Institute as proof that she holds the right views (while some of my colleagues who are also nearing retirement age still see themselves as martyrs). No, my section head, like me, sees her job at the Institute as a profession and a source of income, so she gives it her all, and on top of that she has three children, so she and her husband have to hustle to make ends meet.

The studio apartment assigned to me looks almost the same as my office, which makes sense given that the building has the same setup. The rooms where we sleep are no different from those of our clients, except that, unlike them, we're allowed visitors. The larger apartments, created by joining several offices, are at the very end of the hallway, and that's where the families live. There are cameras here, too, though we all cover them up with pieces of paper, which the system technicians quietly tolerate.

"Rita had nothing. Nothing at all but the head on her shoulders," I tell my clients (the fresh ones, who've only been here a month), meanwhile thinking: Unlike all of you, supported by your families, with the daughters and wives of your sons propping you up, so let's see some results. At which point one of the clients raises his hand to say he saw Rita's portrait in the office of the Institute director. An informant. Thanks to him, we know MK lied about abstaining from porn, because our informant caught him with some behind the wardrobe in their bedroom. I reply, "Naturally. There's a portrait of Rita in every office," and I'm surprised he hasn't noticed, though maybe he has and it's just an awkward attempt to get my attention, so without missing a beat I plow right ahead with my story about Rita in her school days: "Rita sits in a corner of the playground, watching the girls show off for the boys. She challenges the class beauty to a fistfight after school, and after being punched in the face and falling on the asphalt the girl with the split chin is on the receiving end of one of Rita's first-ever lectures. At first, the word among the teachers is 'Rita's a handful.' In her teen years it advances to 'behavioral problems' when at a school dance Rita asks the vice-principal what she's trying to achieve with her terrible makeup: she doesn't have pimples, so is she trying to cover up her age, and doesn't she realize that as an educator she's responsible for modeling certain behavior?"

Two months prior to that, Rita threw a rock through the window of a summer school classroom where a group of adolescent boys were masturbating over pictures of naked women; then, when one of them ended up in the hospital with a concussion, she climbed into his room from the balcony and wrote on the wall in red marker: *I feel sorry for your mom.*

Once the Movement became famous, the boy's mother told the story with pride. At the time, however, she made sure that Rita was thrown out of school.

"Her teachers were well aware what she was up to," I tell my clients, noting that even the so-called progressive educators of the Waldorf schools had no sympathy for Rita's message. (Her mother thought it would be different there, but quickly came to recognize her trust had been misplaced.) As the Waldorf principal so famously put it: "Your daughter's behavior is more than mere boyish mischief." He hit the nail on the head. The faculty had been trained to deal with ordinary bullying, but this?

At this point in the story I pause, raising my eyebrows, and MK calls out, "How could it be boyish mischief if she was a girl?"

"Exactly," I say to MK. "You just earned yourself a little plus." I continue, turning my attention back to the class.

"Rita's reputation quickly spread beyond her hometown. And there were plenty of women in Manhood Watch who didn't even know her name, yet still tried to explain away her actions as the result of an inferiority complex."

I project a series of photographs of Rita onto the wall while my clients dutifully take notes. The classroom is so full we had to bring chairs in from the kitchen. The unusually high turnout may be because it's been raining all day, so even the men who normally play soccer on Tuesday afternoons came today instead of Thursday.

"She looks a lot better there than she does on the one in the director's office," says the informer, commenting on a picture of Rita from the time of her first terrorist attack. A few other clients stifle a laugh. The sign of a guilty conscience. I try to picture OP, aka the fake Ondřej Pěkný, when the Institute staff brought him in, wondering what he looked like when they loaded him into the van at home; or did they pick him up on his way home from work and just mail the family a notice, or was it arranged with the family in advance, and did he scream in the patrol van, and if he did, how loud were his screams?

I project a photo of Rita in a nursery school sandbox (hair tousled from constantly pulling off her knitted cap), Rita in a line of girls standing to attention (before a volleyball tournament?), Rita in a swimsuit—here my clients laugh out loud, and I laugh along with them, because not only has it been ages since anyone wore a swimsuit like that, but the whole idea of fashion has collapsed, and just the thought that it used to be tied to a person's status in society is laughable at this point.

The clients studiously continue taking notes as they watch a loop of captioned photographs of Rita (to my irritation I notice the right corner of the projection spills over onto the wall with the first-aid cabinet). I took on this workshop after the husband of the previous instructor, an Institute old hand nicknamed "Gorilla," got an attractive job offer, and Gorilla moved away with him and their children to Warsaw. Now she holds the same position in the Institute there.

The new clients are always tentative at the start of a workshop, which is understandable, given that it's an unfamiliar environment, plus they have to concentrate. So I tell them it's like the first day of school, their first date with a girl, or their first flight on a supersonic jet, complete with the jitters and the psychological leap into the unknown that comes with seeing a woman for the first time, meaning a woman as a being whose value, and therefore attractiveness, doesn't depend on her age and appearance. Of course this is something they should have known a long time ago, and most of the men do, so I want them to start by feeling good that they're catching on, although what comes as naturally as breathing to Institute graduates can still be quite difficult for new clients, in spite of whatever ideological work they've done on themselves before they come, outside the Institute's walls (thanks to the Movement, the Movement, and, once again, the Movement). Most of them have to learn these new habits the same way they learned to ride a bike or swim, and one of the reasons I make this comparison is that, just like with swimming or riding a bike, they never forget their training after their stay at the Institute. The patrol vans bring back any recidivist cases, and the first place they go is the intensive care unit. It isn't only relatives who call for the pickups, but often the men themselves: "I feel it coming on again," they report over the phone from home, and we're on our way.

The clients sit in a circle, naked (tracksuits folded in a stack), while I'm in my usual baggy pale-blue outfit (gray from so many washings). I start by having them loosen up physically (shaking out their legs and doing the "teacup" rotation with their arms), and also leave a little time for casual conversation.

Then, using precisely formulated questions, I ask the clients to express in their own words what it is that they find attractive in a woman. The majority (who only regurgitate what they've been taught) say intelligence, kindness, a sense of humor, integrity, and dependableness. A minority (touchingly sincere or total morons) say beauty and youth. And a few, proactively, just straight-out describe the qualities that make a woman a woman. After the introduction comes Phase Two, also known as Rehearsal Studio.

Assuming they've read the materials they were given on being admitted (a thick folder with the Institute's logo, which they pore over in their dorm rooms for weeks), the clients know this is coming, but given that everyone who passes through the course is bound by an oath of silence, the actual contents of Rehearsal Studio come as a surprise, and I start the whole thing off, as usual, with pictures: photographs of naked women, alluring in an Old World way, projected on the wall. I rotate through them, one by one, at thirty-second intervals, and as a roar of surprise erupts in the room, I urge the men to relax. Only in this frame of mind can things be revealed for what they truly are, and though our clients are subjected to harsh punishments for unauthorized use of pornography, in a controlled form such as this it can serve as entry-level instructional material.

Because while this group of naked men have already been through a thing or two in their first few days at the Institute, this is the moment when their reeducation starts for real.

"Everything up to this point has been warm-up, gentlemen," I say (I can't even count how many batches of clients I've been through this with by now), and I should stress that this memoir of mine is the first time anyone has described this practice in written form, because now the Institute can be confident of its position, and the graduates of our program can speak openly about their experience with reeducation, so that soon it will no longer be necessary to keep any of our practices secret. Another one of my goals in writing the memoir is to inspire those regions that haven't yet made as much progress in the ways of the New World.

So then: I observe the men closely as their initial confusion on being confronted with pornographic photos quickly gives way to a string of erections, each one acting as a trigger for the next (we know mass erections have a cathartic effect, but a special team of ours is still trying to ascertain the exact mechanism). In a few minutes, nearly every man in the room is hard—the whole thing happens so fast I barely have time to enter it in their individual charts. For the sake of completeness: we define *erection* as "the penis in a state of readiness for application of a condom." Once the atmosphere is sufficiently relaxed (the room is in near darkness, I stimulate the men verbally) and the clients feel at home in the new setting, I make a racy joke or two about condoms, and then we get down to business.

I switch the projector to a new set of photos. Now, instead of smiling girls with large breasts and shapely bottoms, a succession of older women's bodies goes parading past—no retouching or any sort of Old World synthetic enhancement: no skin smoothening, hip narrowing, breast enlargement—

and even without turning to look, I can tell the new loop isn't nearly as popular and the men are disappointed. I hear grumbling behind my back as I adjust the focus to make the images as sharp as possible. Because the key is in the details. The old women's figures are models of ampleness compared to the ones before them—swollen breasts, wrinkled skin, rolls of fat—and when I turn up the lights, even the clients with weak eyesight can clearly see that the hair they thought was platinum blonde is actually gray. Next come the shots of women with gray pubic hair, and I observe the clients from the front again, taking note of whose erection fades and how quickly, and as a handful of men sit with their members completely shriveled, I roar "Shame!" at the top of my lungs, and a deathly silence falls over the room.

Now comes Phase Four. The men are in shock, and that's what we build on. They're disgusted, they feel deceived and made fools of. Instead of talking about what's going on with their bodies, they want to theorize about the Institute's methods. They try to dispute, but all their arguments are biological drivel, so after allowing them to blow off steam awhile (let them speak their piece before Phase Four, the section head stresses to every new instructor), I shout: "Do you eat with your hands at home?"

It's a rhetorical question, so you know what their answer will be, and if I wanted, at this point I could take advantage of my ideological superiority and launch into a monologue on civilization and how completely unnatural it is: instead of eating "naturally" with our hands and "naturally" allowing people with disabilities to die, instead of "naturally" chasing down thieves with a knife and "naturally" leaving elderly and unproductive members of society to fend for themselves, we willingly cultivate ourselves to be humane, in opposition to our natural tendencies. And we're right to be proud of that.

"Yes, it goes against nature," I proclaim. I have their attention more than I did a moment ago, since half the clients think I'm confirming their beliefs, while the other half are wondering what I'm up to. "How are you doing for contraception, gentlemen?" I ask, and my aim here is not to come back to the rubbers I joked about before but to find out which of them has unprotected sex if their partner isn't using anything. Almost nobody ever gives an answer.

"Your shriveled cocks are a punch in the eye to European humanity," I roar. There was a time when I took pleasure in the commotion this usually caused.

I write frantically in the gaps between my shifts and during the breaks in my workshops. As my clients return from lunch (even before the extermination of European livestock, steamed broccoli with caraway seeds was one of their least favorite meals), I take note of the way they're all impatiently squirming in their chairs, since we normally start right on time—a few in the front row even ostentatiously cough.

By now, everyone in my department knows I'm writing something, so I assume others know too, though my section head hasn't asked me about it yet. Still, I expect the question to come any day now, and every day I polish my defense.

"In the Old World, pink clothing was seen to be soiling boyhood as if it were menstrual blood," I shout, then add, lowering my voice, "whereas boys' clothing for girls was deemed acceptable." I go on: "Intellectually minded girls would wear boys' clothing to call attention to their inner qualities, a way of thinking which Rita in her homework referred to as," and here again I raise my voice, "tumorous." When the client by the window calls out without raising his hand to ask if anyone in Rita's family had cancer, I wheel on him: "Out, now!"

He rises without hesitation and patters over to the door. Just under fifty, with tousled gray wisps of hair on an otherwise bald head due to excessive testosterone, the man makes it clear, by the way he throws up his hands and the look on his face, that he feels he's been wronged, and he's entitled to feel that way.

The section head has called me in to talk about this before. "Be careful not to be too unpredictable," she said. "You know how much our clients pay to be here with us.

There's no need to overdo it."

"Half my colleagues are off in the capital, celebrating the anniversary of Rita's first speech in Europarliament. I haven't had a day off in a month," I noted. "I'm always more prone to outbursts when I'm overworked."

The section head nodded in sympathy.

When the client I ejected returns to the classroom after his assigned time of "disgrace" out in the hall, I hear the sound of synchronized male panting from the workshop being led by my colleague next door.

At the end of our session, I assign the men their homework. They each have to pick up a poster in the library. I make them recite the rules, then dismiss them for free-time activities in the yard. The chairs creak as the men gather up their things and shuffle out the door: the well-socialized ones in clusters; the ones who excel, the problem cases, and the informants by themselves. I end the seminar a bit early today. My eyes are burning and my voice is hoarse. I decline the invitation for a smoke from my colleague, who last time talked my ear off.

After a quick read-through of letters from several clients and reviewing a few self-criticisms, I open my memoirs to where I left off.

Now that we have universal contraception and sexual intercourse no longer fulfills a reproductive function, the preference for labia without gray pubic hair is just an outmoded prejudice.

My mother's mother's mother's mother wrote all her shopkeeper's notes (she owned a small haberdashery in a county seat) with a goose quill dipped in a pot of ink. I don't know why, but whenever I hear the phrase "gray pubic hair" I picture her, but without clothes, in a photograph from our family album.

If, once upon a time, the attraction of copulating with a woman was the yoke of evolution, harnessed to the age of her vagina, this evolutionary shortcut has long since become a meaningless behavior, strictly for show.

Regardless of my mother's mother's mother's mother's appearance (a middle-class woman with a tightly wound bun and a grubby skirt), I wish I had her quill and ink, because to write about matters so unalloyedly human on the cloud, even though it's been normal for decades now, feels inappropriate, like instead I should be chiseling it into rock, or stamping it onto credit cards emblazoned with Rita's likeness.

That state of mind keeps coming back, yes, the delirium of being drunk on victory, and unprofessional as it may be, there are times when the price of passion is sheer irrationality, and the whole class is emotional along with me now, the men reading my lips as eager to understand, perhaps, as those Rita spoke to from her soul so many years ago. All those so-called women "agents" eager to extinguish the flames of their femininity, terrified, and rightfully so, that with age it would be denied them.

I begin Phase Four: "Time for the labia tour," I say. The men pair up and I hand each twosome a folder of photographs with vaginas of every age group, bristling with all colors of hair. I introduce the subject of "the habituality of sexual stimuli"—how else?—with a joke about blondes from Old World days, relying on the outmoded belief in the lesser intelligence of women with pale-colored hair.

What I'd really like to do is scream at my assigned group, "We're going to whip you into shape like the hounds you are!" But instead I just smile.

Given the success rate of my seminar, my colleagues sometimes hand their more difficult cases over to me, though it still makes me nervous when the men swing their legs in their chairs, even if they don't do it as much now as they did when I was just starting out. The clients have made a lot of progress since then, too, and the dunces we used to get five or ten years ago are more the exception nowadays.

The classroom is as quiet as a cathedral. My charges are as fired up as I am. They are fascinated by the folded landscape of vulvas with their irregular blossoms, each one differing in its secrets, its center and right-left balance; some symmetrical like faces, others utterly asymmetrical, like individuals with one eye shut, like a person with a freckle over her upper lip.

The jokes I toss out during my presentations

can sometimes backfire on me, and the other day my smoking buddy confirmed something I had long believed, namely that the reason my clients relapse so rarely is because of my sense of humor, and the only thing that distinguishes my sense of humor from a flesh-and-blood assistant is it doesn't make espresso for me.

"In the Old World," I go on, "in the Old World, gentlemen, half of these labias' owners were told to go for plastic surgery and the rest were told to fuck off." When I ask which of the women in this album is ripe for plastic surgery now, in the New World, not a single client raises his hand (the timeless beauty of the women's vulvas has clearly taken the wind from their sails). "So, you see," I add dryly.

Phase Five covers more than just the genitals: the area from the belly down to the knees, to be precise. To prepare, the men masturbate in advance over randomly selected photos from the albums lying open on their laps.

As I ponder how best to describe the Phase Five workshop, I can see the sun setting outside my study windows behind the building that houses the client dorms. I see the lights come on one by one as the guards make their evening rounds, while my other colleagues are away on holiday in the capital, celebrating the anniversary of Rita's speech in Europarliament. I wish them well, and envy them. But someone has to hold down the fort.

"When I look at a woman, I still see mostly ass—tits and ass. Even after three months' treatment, I couldn't care less about her inner complexity as a person," MK scrawled in his confession. This self-criticism is the one I decide to quote, out of all the mountains I've read recently, and not just once but twice, since it's so typical of the Old World and leads nicely into a description of my consultation work.

In the evenings, I make the rounds of clients like MK, and consult with them on an individual basis about their problems with reeducation. The dormitory number for each client is indicated in the top right corner on the first page of their file. In MK's case, it's the rear wing of Pavilion C, where they stored the hides in the days when the building was a meatpacking plant, and to judge from the odor it was never properly aired out.

The language we use in the promo, for the women who visit the Institute on open-door days to have a look around the place where their men will become people, is "We'll raise the IQ of your husband's penis," and if they give us a questioning look, we add, "To 130 at least—satisfaction guaranteed," and slip a brochure in their hand.

At this point, due to the smell from the hides, the women are usually holding their nose with the hand that isn't full of our promotional materials and a foldout map of the Institute (you'd be totally lost by the time you got to Pavilion F without it), and muttering about what an inhumane environment they have to send their husband to (they should see how it used to look before the Institute took over: hooks, tracks, pulleys, fridges full of rotting meat). Of course they know that they don't have to, but that's like telling someone, "It's up to you if you want to have a better life," so only the most hardheaded ones pass it up (and some of them call for a van a few weeks later anyway—it isn't the woman's fault if her man's stuck in his Old World ways; that's what the Institute is here for).

The clients only complain about the smell from the hides the first few days. A person gets used to it, unlike noise, so they're better off than the clients in the dorms above the canteen, with not only the rattle of pots and pans and the beep of convection ovens, but trucks delivering raw materials and revving their engines underneath the windows at all hours.

I head over to the sleeping rooms to find MK, and even though in his last self-criticism he requested to be reassigned to a male instructor, to help get rid of his obsessive thoughts of sex with his current instructor, who's female, I know from years of praxis that he probably has some more practical reason for wanting to meet with me than discussing that. (Some clients think if I let them use my lighter and show interest in how their kids are doing in school, it means they won't have to bother so much with making their beds.)

MK sits in his room, writing at the desk

(each room has just one shared desk, so clients write their letters and self-criticism in shifts). I run my eyes over the furnishings (they smashed the lamp last week, and water has been dripping into a bucket in the corner since the scoundrels on the fourth floor flooded the washroom, and of course the plumbing crew is out of town at Rita's celebration). Posters of old women hang on the walls above the beds, and there are oranges on the nightstands—dessert from yesterday's dinner.

MK sits with his back to me, dressed in his bathrobe, his hair a mess. I've already decided, if he brings up the fact that they don't have any mirrors again, I'll turn around without a word and march straight back to my office.

Startled, he stands to attention, looking me in the eye.

"How many instructional pamphlets did you study last week?" I ask, then wait while he reels off the titles. If asked, clients are also required to summarize relevant passages.

"How about training?" I add once he's through.

I tip my head toward the poster of the old woman.

Masturbation is permitted, for a limited period, as part of our reeducation program. In fact it's required, but only with the use of approved materials.

"Like her looks?" I ask.

MK nods, but doesn't lift his eyes from the floor. (The sleeping-room floors are covered with an optimistic hue of orange linoleum. The shade of the wardrobe reminds me of sirloin, which may have more to do with why I smell meat than the hides they used to store in here.)

"Do you like her looks? Answer me."

The clients choose the posters themselves. We issue new ones in the Institute library every Monday, so Mondays are busier than other days, when the men are just borrowing and returning instructional materials.

The models for the photographs are mature beauties, aged sixty and up, chosen by our people at random off the street. The women who take off their clothes are paid, and as per the contract they sign with the Institute, their faces are covered with black tape.

"You've got it hung a bit crooked," I say, trying to get MK talking.

He's been cooped up in here four months now and has hardly made any progress. The poster, one of the materials we use to train clients in the principles discussed in our coursework, is a celebration of a woman rich in experience, an epic on the theme of maturity and a fully lived life: the woman's belly sags from childbirth (a mother, workshop of miracles), with a scar running diagonally across the right side, probably from a botched appendectomy (this woman knew more about life than MK could ever have imagined). Her crotch is hidden in shadow, but not in order to hide any bloodstain on her panties. My guess is she hasn't had to suffer through menstruation for a good few years now. I am happy for her, and MK must be glad as well. Sexual intercourse with a woman in menopause is more hygienic, and masturbating to a poster of an old lady eliminates the possibility of being disturbed by fantasies of suddenly gushing blood.

The only thing arranged about the portraits for the Institute is the models have to be standing up; once they're paid, they can do whatever they want. Assuming, of course, they're interested in the extra income. Two-thirds of women refuse. In which case our photographer politely thanks them and continues down the street, taking her portable studio with her.

"I came late," says MK after a long silence. He steps up to the poster and jabs a finger at the folds on the woman's belly. "It won't work," he says. "I just can't get off to a woman that old." Honestly, I expected the problem to be the scar. Only a pervert gets off on suffering, but who's bothered by motherhood?

"In your last self-criticism, you talked about desiring coitus with your seminar instructor, and asked to be reassigned to a man. Is this woman's loose skin the reason you desire your instructor?" I ask flat out. At this rate, the only person he's going to lay is himself, on a bed in solitary, but I give him one more chance.

"So the only reason you can't get off is because this person"—now it's my turn to point to the rolls on her belly—"brings other beings into the world? Are you frustrated that, unlike her, you'll never be able to give birth? Do you feel like she's lording it over you?

"Whip it out!" I shout. He's been standing there the whole time like a bump on a log. "Let's go," I add, but there's no need. He heard me the first time: he lowers his track pants, exposing a penis tufted with a furry clump of gray. Our clients aren't issued underwear. Over the course of the average stay in our reeducation program, they would put it on and take it off at least a million times, so we decided it was best to just drop it altogether.

I take his penis in my hand and rub it between my fingers. No erectile dysfunction. Right away it gives a little hop. I let go and it swings back toward his sac. It's disregard for the treatment, that's all. He rejects the Movement's ideas, either because he's too lazy to learn anything new or because his brain is so eroded by porn his penis doesn't know how to react to a non-synthetic female form.

"What do you mean you came late?" I ask as he pulls his pants back up.

"By the time I got to the library on Monday," says MK, "this was the only one left. The other guys took them all before I could get there. I had to mop the hall."

He helplessly throws up his hands. From here on in, I go by the manual. I've got half a mind to just play him the recording and take a break for a smoke, but I have to write up our conversation and the summary is going to be entered in his file, so I continue:

"What is the purpose of your reeducation?" I ask, as if he were a schoolboy. MK goes back to staring at the ground.

"For me to view women as human beings, not cunts."

"And what does that mean?"

MK runs his eyes over the linoleum. I leave the vulgarity on his part without comment.

"Taking an interest in them as people, not cunts."

Another client peeks his head into the bedroom. MK throws him a glance and the head withdraws.

"What does that mean?" I ask again, with greater emphasis.

I dream of a New World in which the male population is fully schooled in the ideas of the Movement, a world in which the dialogue I'm having now with MK will no longer be needed, and I know that time will come, but meanwhile someone has to push to get us there: my colleagues and I in the classrooms of thousands of Institutes just like this, along with all the work going on out in the field.

"That I don't believe they lose value with age."

"What else?" I bark, hoping to get it over with fast.

"That my interest in women isn't determined by their biological features, but by the compatibility of our attributes, by their personality, outlook, and vision of our shared life."

I sit down. My feet hurt. I drum my fingers on the desktop.

"Old World porn, in brief," I order, stretching my legs. "The basics," I add, suppressing a yawn. "Go."

"Masturbation with porn turns human beings into things. When a man uses porn, it reinforces his view of women as objects." He pauses. "Whether he means to or not."

"Excellent," I say. "So porn is what?"

"Filth," he fires back instantly.

"And what does it get you?"

"Solitary, quarantine, the icebox, death."

I indicate in his file that he's answered the questions correctly. His knowledge is sufficient, it's his praxis that's lagging, but that's always the case. It's the same with languages. It's easier to read than to speak. Conversation is an art form, and we expect nothing less of our clients than for them to master the art of life, human life. This isn't about rattling off some memorized phrases in Latin. It takes time, and you can't panic. Panic is for novices. Carried away with enthusiasm, they expect clients to run like clockwork right from the start, and then get disappointed when they don't. They alternate between blaming themselves and blaming the clients, forgetting that the clients aren't here for them, but the other way around. For us the payoff comes when our clients behave properly back on the outside.

Reeducation takes time, and despite all my

experience I still sometimes push too hard. Mainly when I forget that every man we work with is different.

"Try now," I tell MK. "One more time."

I lean forward, but he's already untying his giant pants himself (he must have also showed up late to the laundry room, so that the only size they had left was extra-large). He takes hold of his penis and, fixing his gaze on the poster, begins to masturbate, standing up.

"Lie down, make yourself comfortable," I say, looking out the window. The only sound I hear in reply is sighing. Gradually, the sighs get louder and louder, and when they come to a stop, I know my visit has been worth it.

I'll tell the maintenance women to replace the desk with a new one. My guess is it used to be in the corner, where the bucket is now, and the surface got warped by the water from the flooded washroom upstairs. A new desk would also be helpful to me, since I'm the one who has to decipher the clients' chicken scratch, a job I wouldn't wish on anyone, and with the desktop rippled the way it is, chicken scratch is all you get.

"So, how was it?"

MK gives me a smile, but I know he's too proud to thank me, and I don't expect him to. The improvement in his condition is satisfaction enough for me. I indicate the progress in his file while he pulls his pants up over his belly button, the same way my father used to do.

"See you Thursday," I say. Thursdays we have workshop, and for several sessions already MK's group has been on Phase Five, which I'll describe in more detail shortly.

My next stop is a visit to OP. Though I really should see my clients every day, my colleagues and I do it once a week at most, and the section head lets us get away with it.

Like any other agency, some of the Institute's regulations exist only on paper, since it stands to reason they were drawn up before we began operations, just as it also stands to reason that praxis always differs from the initial conception in some way—in this case by the fact that we have less time than our predecessors imagined. They got carried away when it came to certain aspects of our work, and overestimated our capacity.

Out in the hallway, I greet a few informants heading back from shop to the dorms to enjoy an hour or so of personal free time before dinner.

OP is waiting for me on the bench in the hall outside his room. He offers his right hand, but I just leave it hanging. We don't shake hands with clients until they show visible improvement. OP's constant questions about what's expected of him have some of my colleagues suspecting him of being a spy, and I wouldn't want to be in his shoes when he suffers the consequences. When it comes to spying we don't mess around, especially since the uprising. Besides, if he has questions he should address them to me, his guard, or the section head and not go flagging down our overworked doctors and nurses in the hallways whenever he gets the urge.

"You know very well under what circumstances we perform electrotherapy," I say, feeling uncomfortable. Which is how *he* should be feeling right now, since every little kid knows that—it may be just a saying, but here at the Institute it's literally true. The kids in our company crèche love to play with the old, discarded electrotherapy helmets.

"We serve you, not the other way around. Your correction is in your own interest. It's all in your hands."

I keep an eye on him to see how he reacts. With some "problem clients" the only real problem is they've got nowhere to go. With nothing to look forward to on the outside, they've managed to adapt to life here in the Institute (usually it's members of the porn mafia, who we have a running battle with), operating under the misguided belief that they're somehow special, so electroshock treatment can't happen to them. But watching OP, I get the feeling this isn't the case. He looks too smart for that.

"You have to put an end to your internal doubts once and for all, and given your history, I recommend you don't delay."

He grins. He knows we're thoroughly acquainted with his "history," but my mention of it has caught him off guard. The first part of every client's file is their personal history, and on the outside OP was a member of Manhood Watch. I'm not surprised that my more impulsive colleagues, especially the ones with low self-confidence, can't let him off the hook. There are times when even I feel my hand start to tingle and I'd like to slap him right in the face, even though I know that sort of behavior is unacceptable. In short, OP is ripe for probation. It's either/or. Either he shapes up and puts an end to his inner resistance, or he gets sent to Pavilion F.

My colleagues return from the celebration of the anniversary of Rita's speech in Europarliament brimming with enthusiasm and shopping bags full of souvenirs, which they decorate their offices with, then give the rest away. The kitchen is mobbed with takers at every break. Anyone who imagines the celebration as a parade of women carrying pictures of Rita, allegorical floats, and adulatory clichés, however, would be mistaken. In fact it featured a slate of debates on current topics, and the whole thing was organized by graduates of our Institutes. My colleagues mention the names of a few former clients of ours. I remember some of them were not only ignorant, but hardcore cases, involved in acts of outright sabotage. Next to them, my troubles with MK and OP are laughable, a common example of the difficulties involved in reeducation, of the resistance and lack of understanding we have to overcome. If the only problem is a lack of understanding, education is generally enough; if they actively resist, electrotherapy may also be used as a last resort, as well as other forceful means, which I will get to later on.

I sit drinking coffee in the kitchen with my colleagues, watching a recording of one of the featured speakers at the celebration, a man who starts by citing the now-momentous words: "Up to now, the entire history of our celebrated Euro-American humanism has avoided the unequal order underlying the Old World like the Devil avoided the cross." He was brought here in one of our patrol vans, without even his wife's consent, straight from "dinner with a female companion." He and his coworkers had gone to an illegal house of prostitution after closing a business deal. They were dragged out of the building and into the street, shirttails and flushed cheeks exposed for all the world to see.

Today, one of our Institutes is housed in that very building ("symbolically," as they say), and in his emotional address, the cured man says of that day: "There I was, ready to dump my seed into that woman like a bucket, when two angels appeared," and while it may seem like brownnosing to call our ambulance workers angels, that would only be true if it was a false confession of guilt. But the man at the podium in the capital is tearing up, and besides, he's already passed the final exam, so it isn't as if he has to curry favor with anyone.

"My perspective on life has fundamentally changed," says the man, reading from a piece of paper. ("Fraud!" a member of Manhood Watch screams from the crowd. They're so pathetic they can only interpret his statement as the product of a rigged "political process.") "My perspective on life has fundamentally changed, and I owe it to you too, Mirka." He invites his wife onstage to thunderous applause. "Your beauty comes from within. How could I have been so blind?" says the man, now choking up. One of the open secrets about his case is that his wife wanted to divorce him over the incident with the prostitute, but when she came to visit him at the Institute, our section head persuaded her to give him one more chance. Today they're one of our prize couples.

The Movement takes care of couples like them. They shuttle them around to speak at public meetings with women moderators who introduce the men, saying, "This is what a man who's gone through reeducation looks like." Then the man runs out onstage to applause and declares, "I'm living proof that men can change their 'nature.' The problem is the nature of the Old World, not men." He's then followed by a series of other men who've gone through reeducation, and they all tear up onstage together, and the public TV newscasters report that ninety percent of the male population is now civilized, and Institute graduates with YouTube channels report on it, too (but with more humor), "testifying" to their own transformation, and Manhood Watch can rage all they want, but all they've got against the Movement is gossip.

"We'll put an end to this whole silly dance of animal courtship within a decade," Rita declared in her speech to Europarliament, and although it hasn't happened quite that fast, the moment is now within reach.

Listening to the video with my eyes closed, the snatches of speech sound as if they're coming from a distance. From another continent, where the Movement is still at war but we have the upper hand. And when I picture the defeat of our adversary, I see a meadow filled with human beings, and it's immediately clear who's a man and who's a woman, only now in a whole new way.

On the night shift, I make the rounds of the client dormitories. Silence reigns over the empty hallway, broken only by the occasional buzz of a fluorescent light. The atmosphere is more boarding school than detox, and I note to myself that it also has some prisonlike qualities to it, though our spas give clients the positive feeling they're cleansing themselves of deeply ingrained atavisms.

I take my snack from my pocket—an apple grown by clients in the orchard adjoining the courtyard of the meatpacking plant, a proverbial "garden of cultivation." The concept spread quickly from Institute to Institute, since the more self-sufficient we are, the more money it saves our donors, like the pre-Christmas markets in the Institute parking lot (the patrol vans park along the side on those days, by the fence that encircles the main yard), which offers handicrafts fashioned by clients in their free-time courses, and we also open our doors on those days to children whose dads are in here.

As I chew my apple, I ponder whether to send OP and MK to solitary if they don't start to cooperate, or whether to go with electrotherapy instead, and though I've warned MK about transferring him to Pavilion F (and he's well aware what that means), in OP's case electroshock seems unavoidable, given that only a tiny minority of Manhood Watch members manage to get through their time here without it.

In short, there are times when the only way to combat stubbornness is a stream. A stream of cold water, a stream of insults, a stream of electricity. A stream of light, on the other hand, is just an instrument for seeing, I think to myself as I open the door to the sleeping room, letting in a cone of light from the hallway, and sit down on my first client's bed, which is right next to the door.

I double-check the number of both the room and the client (printed on a slip inserted into the nightshirt hanging on the footboard of the bed), as well as the card I carry around with me on my rounds in the back right pocket of my guard's uniform. Everything matches up, this is my man. He's nearing the time of his final exam.

Clients in this situation like to say they're already one foot out the door, bragging to anyone who will listen and asking their wives to request their release, even though they're still awaiting the final decision. To their minds, it's just a matter of passing the final exam, but whether or not they get to take it is up to the guard. I decide for the ones who fall under my charge, and the purpose of my nightly rounds is to help me make that decision.

I'm careful not to wake anyone in the room except the man I've come to see. As I lower myself onto the bed, it gives a little squeak, so I pause a moment, sitting still. Then, with a practiced motion, I pull off his blanket. Prior to their final exam, clients are required to sleep on their backs. After so many months of drills, they don't even bother to ask why. At this stage of their reeducation, the men have total trust in us. They've learned for themselves that everything we put them through—and almost all of them balk at some point (calling in a lawyer to contest solitary, kicking back when they're hosed with cold water, throwing a fit over a personal search)—that all of the measures we employ are ultimately for their own benefit.

I gently lower the pants of client number five-two-five (at moments like these, I always think how much more complicated it must have been for staff before the ban on wearing underwear), pull on a glove, and gently take hold of his shriveled penis. I pause for a moment, wondering how long this man has been here. I take out my flashlight and shine the light over the bed. In the spot on the wall where OP, MK, and the other men at a lower level of reeducation have their posters of mature models, this man has nothing, which is standard for clients prior to the final exam. I focus a little harder, and yes. Barely noticeable, but it's there: a slightly whiter rectangle left behind on the wall. That means the man has been rotting away in here a good long time (probably had a few regressions, maybe a failed discharge, and who knows, maybe even an outright escape attempt). As I think all this, it only makes me root for the man that much more. I close my eyes and make a wish for him to succeed, and I swear it's not only because it would free up capacity and prevent an increase in our average length of stay, which is the statistic that all the Institutes compare with one another and that women use as a guide in choosing where to send their men. I also wish it personally for myself. Because yes, the stay can be an ordeal for men and it's my duty to minimize how hard it really is, but I've come to know a thing or two over the years, and there are nights when I walk in and the clients' faces are swollen from crying and they scream the names of family members out loud in their sleep.

If I didn't have my right hand around his penis and my left hand in my pocket, where my flashlight is, I would cross my fingers for him for real, not just in my mind, though of course I know it wouldn't help. It's up to him and him alone. I'm only a tool. Like an electricity tester, which, apart from its lack of conductivity, has no qualities of its own.

I grip the penis firmly, going up and down, up and down, running it through the practice drill. It's soft, so far not even a trace of swelling. Just like its owner, the penis is sleeping the sleep of the just. The wail that cuts the silence a moment later isn't from five-two-five, but the client by the window, apparently having a nightmare. I myself wake up in sweat at least once a month, and it always takes a few minutes sitting there for it to sink in that nothing's actually happening to me.

My night terrors come from the hair-raising stories I've heard my colleagues tell. From back in the days when they had a looser regime, with no cameras in the toilets, so the porno mafia were able to plan their uprising for weeks without anyone noticing.

They broke into the dining facilities from the yard (a delivery of fresh baked goods was due in, so the gate was left unlocked), tied up the cooks in the kitchen using their shoelaces (ever since then, clients are only issued moccasins), armed themselves with kitchen knives, and then, instead of taking the route past reception to escape (did they know there were security guards with guns there?), they headed for the section head's office, where they demolished the furniture, stabbed the section head, then declared over the internal PA (normally used to issue instructions to the floor): "Long live the end of this disgusting experiment." No sooner had the rebels made their declaration than some staff alerted by one of the cooks who managed to get away burst into the office and shot the men with .27 caliber pistols. The director's instructions were explicitly to "disable," but when one of the women saw Rita's portrait trampled on the ground, broken glass everywhere, the frame smashed to bits—in short, desecrated—something in her snapped and she unloaded the entire magazine into the rebels.

Today, we all agree the massacre should have been avoided. The men involved should have been detained and placed in solitary. It was a squandered opportunity. An opportunity for them to mend their ways, and ultimately, for them to pass the final exam. I mean, what better advertisement could we have than the reeducation of porno mafia members who tried to stage a revolt?

Five-two-five's penis comes this close to slipping out of my hand. An error of inattention, and a moment later it happens again, this time completely (as I picture the scene with Rita's portrait again). I lift his member carefully from the curly hairs of the scrotum, the man mutters something unintelligible, I look at my watch. The mandatory five minutes are up, and his penis, despite stimulation, is still soft as an earthworm. Cheered by the outcome, I pull the client's pants up over his member, cover him with a blanket, and, almost as if he knew it was over and he'd passed with flying colors, he heaves a contented sigh and rolls over to face the wall. I make my exit, pulling off the rubber glove and tossing it in the wastebasket next to the door in the hall. I pull a new one out of my sack and reach for the door handle of the dorm room across the way.

Client three-oh-eight is on the bed beneath the window. I check the number on his bed one more time to be sure. He lies on his back, smiling.

I'm familiar with the dreams that clients have from their self-criticism and our regular consultations. This one is lying so still on his bed he looks like a picture, and his file contains nothing but praise (hardworking, understanding, active, gets along well with others). I remember him from the seminar. He was the one who asked me about Rita's family. "From the age of three, she lived only with her mother. Her father had no contact with them," I answered him. Manhood Watch tried to reduce the Movement's social origins to the misfortunes of a little girl who couldn't forgive her father for walking out on her, and who was now taking out her rage on others. As if the discovery of a cure for cancer wouldn't count if the scientist had a tumor herself, as if ... suddenly I snap to attention: the moment the darkness outside turns to gray and the first birds begin to chirp, I feel a twitch in three-oh-eight's member. Apparently the dose of rysol that they put in the evening meals of clients scheduled for nighttime exams, so they won't wake up while the guards are handling their penis, wasn't strong enough for this one. He starts squirming around in his bed, and I have to grip his penis more tightly to keep it from sliding out of my hand, and yes, it's still getting bigger. I continue with the procedure. It's my duty to go on for at least three minutes regardless of the response. And, although rarely, it does occur that a penis will give a slight jerk, then drop back down again, as if having changed its mind. That isn't the case with three-oh-eight, unfortunately. He just goes right on wriggling, and though the rysol in his system keeps him from fully waking up, his penis grows steadily larger as he twitches this way and that. I start to worry he might wake the other men, so I clamp my other hand over his mouth, just in case. He turns red in the face, tossing his head. I press down harder, counting the seconds, while his eyeballs roll around beneath his eyelids.

As the darkness turns to gray, I can make out the silhouettes of things inside the room. The place is a mess. Maybe a fight broke out after lights-out. The poster of the model over the client opposite's bed has been torn down and lies crumpled on the floor. I glance around at the others, but except for three-oh-eight, who has no poster since his test is coming up, the rest are hung perfectly straight. The one beneath the window shows a gaunt-looking eighty-year-old, scalp gleaming through a tuft of white hair, sharp-cut features reminiscent of a rat-poison label. A mature beauty, half Grim Reaper, I think to myself. It isn't for nothing they call orgasms "the little death." The best aphrodisiac that exists is knowing you're near the end (they say in war zones people have sex like their lives depend on it). The woman's breasts sag like empty sacks. She gave every last bit of herself to life—and to be moved, to be moved by a woman's fragility, can also have an erotic impact. It did even in the Old World. The Movement just works with it in a new way.

I pull three-oh-eight's pants back over his member, covering him the way he was when

I entered the room, and as I smooth the blanket's edges (the gift of caring for others isn't in contradiction with the Movement), I think about the woman on the poster. Who she is and whether she's still here on this earth or has already departed for whatever it is that comes after death (the Movement has no theory on this), and, if she's still alive, I wonder what her intimate life is like (the Old World denied the desires of elderly women with the vehemence of a Holocaust denier). She probably has a reeducated man at home—not a robot or escort service like most eighty-year-old women had when I was in my youth, but a man who fawns over her. Because old age is just a bridge back to childhood. An unruly client, still in his early reeducation, might sneeringly add: "And childhood's just a hop, skip, and a jump from adolescence—which has always been seen as a turn-on in women, so even an Old World guy ought to be able to get it up for an old lady." Old age marks a return to the defenselessness of our early years, and, now that we're on the subject of childhood, I've got some thoughts on that as well. My mother had a reputation for being a beauty—first they said she is, then they said she was—and meanwhile it was like my father didn't have any looks at all. That was the lie the Old World fed us, and for centuries people swallowed it: women look like, whereas men are and do. Manhood Watch claimed the Movement was just a bunch of women obsessed with how shitty their families had been, to which I say: Those who think are those forced to think by circumstance. It was just an avalanche waiting to happen, and the Movement is what unleashed it. I'm sorry, but people's hang-ups are what resonate with the masses.

Out in the hallway, I remove the rubber glove covered in penis slime. As I toss it in the trash, I wonder why it is that I keep going back in time in my thoughts. Then I realize there are moments in my personal life that might actually come in handy in writing my memoirs.

Back in my office I write *Rejected* in three-oh-eight's file. Thinking about the eighty-year-old model reminds me of my time working at Pornjoy, where they developed all that stuff that was once used in massive quantities not only by men, but also by women of the same age as the women on the posters. I'll keep my fingers crossed for three-oh-eight when he retakes the exam.

Today is the first Wednesday of the month, open-door day. I show the visitors around—women, married couples, and men (more and more older bachelors are now entering treatment of their own free will)—to the canteen, the classrooms, the client dorms, and if anyone is interested, I also take them down to the solitary confinement cells. Back when the Institute was a meatpacking plant, the basement rooms were used to store preservatives, barrels of flavoring, and spare parts for the conveyor belts—all nonperishable items immune to the damp, which clients tend to complain about after their second, third, or fourth month locked away. We sympathize with the fact that it's damp, but not with the complaints, since there are reasons why the men are sent to solitary, and those reasons are reviewed by at least three people—section head, doctor, and guard—as well as the nursing staff.

"My Míša would go out of his mind in here," says a long-legged blonde as I give her the tour. Her knees nearly buckle as she peeks into one of the two cells, both currently vacant, and even though just a moment ago, when I took her through the garden, she was ready to send her husband here next week, it looks like now she's starting to reconsider.

"You said he suggested you get breast implants, which would mean he qualifies for the maximum stay with us." I wonder which illegal clinic he wants to send her to, the lout, since external cosmetic modifications have been illegal for at least five years. Manhood Watch has spent those years bemoaning the fact that procedures now take place in unsanitary and unprofessional conditions (with women being crippled at clinics run by unlicensed doctors out to make a quick buck), but in the Old World, when doctors screwed up a woman's plastic surgery nobody gave two hoots, and what else was a plastic surgery clinic but the Old World in a microcosm.

After the Interior Ministry basement, the second place Rita bombed was a plastic surgery clinic, without hesitation, and I say without hesitation because she blew it up just three days after the ministry. The whole country was gripped with panic. Out of fear for the safety of their employees, most clinics "interrupted operations" within a few days. The doctors just stopped going to work.

"But I'm the one who wants them," the woman replies as I relatch the basement door (my smart card's acting up again). We head up to my office, then I dash out and a minute later come right back with coffee. One for me, one for her. I know from experience the conversation will take at least an hour. An hour for me to convince her, plus another till she signs the papers. And if you asked me what percentage of women who come to the Institute to have their men interned end up in facilities themselves, I would say fifteen plus. Community Centers is what we call the treatment facilities for women.

"It'll give you a chance to relax, Mrs. Ptáčková," I say, handing packets of sugar across the desk. I don't intend to hide anything, it's solely up to her. "While your husband is here being treated for his addiction to porn, you can rid yourself of your addiction to makeup, the ideal of the Old World figure, and your obsession with the size of your breasts," I say as she stirs sugar into her coffee.

I figure she must be from the countryside. It's the only way to explain how she's been getting away with her illegal behavior. In some rural areas, the Old World is still hanging on, tooth and nail. I know from the media as well as from my colleagues, who passed through several villages on their way to the capital for the anniversary of Rita's speech in Europarliament.

"The world doesn't look at you—you look at it." I choose my words carefully. It's important not to moralize, or she might be scared off and not even bring us her husband. Choosing the right words in the midst of so many prejudices is like walking through a minefield. But introducing the New World in a way that will appeal to a woman with no education, you have to forget finesse and take the blunt approach: "For starters, there's nothing wrong with pigging out on sweets,"

I say. Suddenly Mrs. Ptáčková is all ears.

"With a figure like yours, you can do whatever you want. Once Míša completes his re-education, the only thing that will matter to him is what you're like on the inside. Your true self, the richness of your soul, the way you relate to each other. Which means you can finally grow old without worrying, and eat whatever you want, as long as you keep an eye on your health. But that's purely up to you."

The blonde stares silently into her coffee.

"Every Community Center program includes wellness procedures and field trips. The one I'd recommend to you is next to a preserve with natural mineral springs ..."

I remember my own visit there several years ago. The paths in the adjacent park where the residents went for walks between procedures were lined with a rare variety of orange tulips (reportedly a gift from a donor in the Netherlands).

"Does wellness include cosmetics?" asks the blonde. "I've been considering permanent makeup," she adds, and I wonder what kind of backwater she must be from to be thinking about getting something that years ago women in cities paid good money to have removed, and whether diversity is really the right word to describe the diametrically opposed situation between cities and rural areas, or if it's time to bring the term "two-speed Europe" back into style.

In the end we agree that Mrs. Ptáčková, like so many others, will attend the Community Center on an outpatient basis. The Movement has no desire to drag women away from their children, especially not nowadays, when thanks to our efforts their interest in giving birth has increased.

I think what finally tipped the scale was my comment about her husband's young female coworkers, whom she mentioned in passing, setting me up for the smash: "After his stay at the Institute, he won't pay any attention to those girls at the front desk anymore—that I guarantee."

Hearing those words, it was like a weight lifted from her shoulders, and when I told her again that she could eat whatever she wanted, and that the Community Center offered an all-you-can-eat buffet 24-7, she was practically in the bag. Especially when she revealed that the main reason she wanted to get her breasts enlarged was because of the girls at her husband's job.

"You really think he'll still love me when I'm old?" she asked skeptically. It was as if she had slept right through the last decade. She insisted on showing me the bags under her eyes, "to make me understand." She smiled when I told her we didn't have any mirrors. That clinched the deal. After two hours in my office, she walked out in a state of elation.

"I'll drop him off on Wednesday, I promise, right after work."

How many forgotten regions did we still have in this country, like the place where this woman lived? I thought, and I felt a drop of sweat trickle down my back, imagining all the work that still lay ahead of us. Mrs. Ptáčková and I shook hands goodbye, and I escorted her out to the parking lot.

"So what is he going to love about me when I turn fat and old?" she asked as she looked for the keys to her car.

I was so bowled over by the backwardness of her question, I had to steady myself against one of our vans to keep from stumbling.

"Do you really not value yourself at all?" I asked.

I knew it was wrong the moment I said the word *value*, because if she valued herself, she never would have asked such a stupid question, but I managed to wrap things up with a more professional-sounding "The courses here will help you with that" or "You'll figure that out once you're here," since I had other women waiting for me and I was in a rush.

Every open-door day I meet with several women like Mrs. Ptáčková. It kills me every time, and the only thing to do is steel myself with patience. Because when you get right down to it, it isn't the women's fault, and it's our obligation to treat them with understanding.

After Rita bombed the Interior Ministry basement and the plastic surgery clinic, one early morning her team planted explosives in a shopping mall. The only person killed was a night watchman, a standard example of his social class in the Old World (the inside of his dressing-room locker was plastered with pictures of Thai porn), who was torn to shreds. It may sound like I'm using the victim's morality as an excuse for the violence, but the watchman's wife was a victim too (of the morality that she and her husband shared in common), and all this races through my head as I tell Mrs. Ptáčková goodbye and say, "Make sure Míša packs a board game. He'll have lots of free time while he's here." Not only is this a lie, but I doubt Mr. Ptáček will pack his bag himself; more likely his wife will do it, since in the Old World most women fell into the category of "wanting to support" their husbands by doing them these types of favors, explaining it away with statements like, "He's such a mess he doesn't even know where his socks are."

I often arrive at the classroom at the last minute. The hallways here get crowded sometimes, even though the Institute's operations are designed to avoid having different groups cross paths: clients going to work in the kitchen garden take the stairs, while clients on their way to lunch in the ground-floor canteen take the huge elevator that used to carry caged chickens, and yet another group tramps down the maintenance stairs on the side of the building to hypnotherapy, or to the kitchen for a relaxing course in Tajik cuisine (in which case they take the main staircase, installed where they tore out the escalators that used to lead to the conveyor belt).

This morning the patrol vans brought in a new batch of men—four full loads, packed so tightly they were sitting on top of each other. They kept screaming that they weren't refugees, but our section head said they came from a squat out in the woods, and had barricaded themselves in, issuing a string of proclamations from their "outpost of patriarchy," as the media dubbed it, calling for "the overthrow of this dreadful situation," until finally, after a few weeks, our leaders decided the fun and games were over. The Movement's armed response unit accomplished its mission in just three days. If the men had been even slightly less aggressive, most likely our leaders would have just left them out there to die a dignified death in the wild.

On the way from my studio to the classroom where I'll be conducting a Phase Five workshop, I wade through a swarm of red-faced men with beards being herded to registration. It isn't just their grimy, smelly clothes that they have in common with refugees, but their Old World views, and it's no coincidence that Manhood Watch has been recruiting like mad in multicultural communities ever since the Movement began. Egalitarian humanism, the Movement's unsinkable ship, was under fire from the Common Platform of Men of Diverse Cultures, which at the suggestion of their PR advisers was soon renamed the Common Platform of Men and Women of Diverse Cultures, which strictly speaking is everything, which is to say is nothing at all.

The forest men had no real leaders, and as I picked my way through the crew of irate squatters, I knew the members of the CPMWDC must be lighting up the Institute director's cell phone at that very moment to complain about the raid. At times like these the director typically switched off her ringer, to the mischievous delight of all of us here at the Institute.

Meanwhile I had the novices bring the

dummy female torsos out of storage up to the classroom, along with the enlarged photos of women's crotches, that is, the area between the knees and the belly button. Back when I was at Pornjoy, torsos like these were my daily bread.

I know the name Pornjoy doesn't mean anything in the more outlying areas, so I'll offer a brief introduction, though you may have one around the corner that you've been mistaking for an IKEA warehouse.

Working at Pornjoy was like any other temp job, really. I was not yet twenty, looking to earn some cash, and I stumbled across the ad while searching for something about Rita on the internet. It said they wanted a "painter of epoxy surfaces." The building was a barn on the outskirts; from the outside it looked like a warehouse. I entered through the rear for my shifts, and painted the rear ends of female dummies shaped according to the Old World ideal of beauty and programmed with the vocabulary of a five-year-old. Rear ends and torsos. Like the ones here on my desk at the front of the class, which I'm not looking at but across, since I'm taking attendance, and the way the novices set it up, the dummy torsos are between me and my clients, so I'm standing behind a desk covered in artificial flesh.

The twilight of the Old World was an era of animals and artificiality. Bodies were becoming artificial and souls were becoming animal. At a distance of three feet, the Pornjoy dummies, whose breasts, buttocks, and fingertips I painted with several layers of special shellac, were indistinguishable from living women. And in the same way male turkeys will mate with a broom if you put a polyurethane female turkey's head on it, the male temp workers at Pornjoy had sex with not only every new model dummy before it went on the market, but also the torsos, which were nothing more than crotches (hardly anyone in the Old World could afford to buy a full mannequin on an average salary).

Each morning, on arriving, we would be issued our work clothes and change into them at our lockers. ("Drinking water is available from the fountains throughout working hours," I remember still from our training—it's always the most trivial things that stick in my head.) As far as the dummies themselves go, the models that stood the test of time were used as templates and put into serial production. During the year I worked at Pornjoy, the dummies' vocabulary increased from that of a child to the level of a pre-adolescent teen, and while my male coworkers were having sex with dolls that looked like crash test dummies, my eyesight went to pot. I blame it on Rita, since, along with every other mainstream urban young woman at the time, I had just begun to follow her and spent all my spare time reading her work. Of course, plenty of educated young men of my generation called her writings drivel. People don't put two and two together until they're mentally prepared for it. For me the deciding factor was definitely my family environment (my mother's favorite slogan, "Live your dream and never back down") and, like the man at the anniversary celebration of Rita's speech in Europarliament ("There I was, ready to dump my seed into that woman like a bucket, when suddenly I saw angels"), I saw the light one day on our noontime break as I was looking over the shoulder of one of my fellow temps and saw her texting a picture of her genitals to someone. The next day one of the guys I worked with, whom I liked, showed me a picture of her vagina on his phone and asked if I would send him mine, so he could "compare" and "maybe hit me up."

"What's wrong with you?" he yelled when I responded to him with a slap in the face. "Have you got a problem with your pussy?" I slapped him again. He turned and walked away. The Old World would have said, "Emancipation means women don't have to be ashamed of their genitals," or "You won't let a man see what you show every toilet bowl?" And at that moment I realized the Movement's struggle had to be taken to the extreme, and if there was anything I personally could do to contribute, there could be no higher meaning in life for me than that. It was like something asleep inside of me waking up, because to understand the world it isn't enough just to piece together a picture from the fragments—you have to grasp the significance of what you're seeing, and suddenly it was everywhere I looked: porn-addicted men who viewed women as nothing but bodies, as throwaway plastic bags whose contents they couldn't care less about, and aging women lined up outside of sex shops, celebrated by the Old World as proof of emancipation.

Despite the Old World's trumpeting of humanism to death, it still conveniently insisted on animalistic rules of sexuality, pointing to "human nature, which nobody can change." And I say conveniently because in every other aspect of life, nature was treated as having no limits at all, elastic as a piece of chewing gum, utterly malleable by "technology."

My clients in the classroom are grumbling. I've left them unattended too long. Peering between the legs of one of the torsos, I see MK copying notes from the client sitting next to him, probably from a class he missed. He didn't show up last Thursday. We do let slide an absence every now and then, especially since I get the sense he still needs time to think everything through, and especially after my last consultation with him, which ended successfully in his climax, but only after he'd thoroughly slandered the model on his poster.

I ask the clients to pair up, then distribute the torsos. We launched Phase Five last Thursday, so this group should be familiar with the basics by now. There's a stack of labia albums on my desk, which one of the eager novices brought up from storage "just in case" (the pages are laminated to protect from ejaculate), but I'm sure we won't be needing them.

I have a client in front pass out the torsos (one per pair), then ask the men to describe them. Our torsos here, unlike the ones I painted at Pornjoy, show clear signs of deterioration (for every few Institutes there's one common "shop" that specializes in the production of our educational aids). Every torso is a unique, distinctive landscape. I was never really interested in Old World modern art ("You're just too stupid to get it," people would say), but I appreciate the beauty of the New World. Manhood Watch, and now the multicultural parasites of the CPMWDC, like to claim the Movement is "bitter" because it refuses to see beauty as "a value in itself" ("Rehabilitate beauty" is the CPMWDC's appeal, but at this point it's playing second fiddle to the Movement). True beauty is in the marks that life leaves on us, and the female dummy torsos my clients have in front of them have been marked by life in every way imaginable.

"Yes, you dolt, a landscape," I reply in a fit of emotion to a question from a client (after he objects that he missed last week's workshop due to the flu, I apologize). A landscape like the surface of the earth, and though the concept of woman as Gaia could hardly be more foreign to the Movement, the torsos' wrinkled bellies and time-warped thighs are a beauty in themselves, like the age rings on an ancient linden.

In the Old World, when a tree stump was too big for two or three people to wrap their arms around, it was dubbed a monument, whereas the age rings on old women's bodies were viewed as off-putting, and dried plums may go for a higher price than fresh ones, but the moment someone compared a woman's behind to a prune in the Old World it was no longer in demand even if it was for free.

I invite the clients to study the torsos' buttocks. Some shrug with a sly grin; others I can tell are burning with desire. MK smiles, nodding fervently. Evidently his masturbating in my presence was a major breakthrough. He understands the material now and is justifiably proud. It's like anything else in life: what's hard at first over time becomes automatic. I smile back at MK with a friendly nod that he alone understands and remind myself yet again: when clients feel supported, and someone they know and trust acknowledges the progress they've made in their reeducation, we can work wonders.

One after the other, the men take turns caressing the torsos, enumerating their assets, and I'm blown away by the richness of the adjectives they come up with; the comparisons are practically poetic. At moments like these, when I see the results of all the hard work we've put in, I have an urge to walk down the rows and hug them, each and every one. So I move on to our last point more quickly than usual: mass masturbation over the torsos—like a choreographed performance in honor of Rita's speech in Europarliament, the pulling down of pants by the whole group all at once is truly a joy to see. At the end, since we still have time, I call on them one by one, not only asking them questions about the material, but trying to draw out how they feel about their orgasms. The classroom is baking hot and smells like a gym, proof of a job well done, and I close by letting the clients themselves ask questions. They're curious how the instructional aides are made, so I talk briefly about the shop where the torsos are produced, and caught up in my own euphoria, I offer to lead a field trip there at the end of the summer, assuming we can get enough clients to sign up and my section head approves.

For the first time in ages I finish on time, which gives me a moment to stop by my studio before my evening rounds of the dorms. My mother sometimes teases me in her emails that I traded in our comfortable two-bedroom flat for a "rabbit hutch," and how am I supposed to think about anything but work when I live in a meatpacking plant? She's judging me unfairly, I think, even as I'm sorting through my clients' files in my head at that very moment. The Institute is at near-full capacity. We had to put the refugees in unfurnished rooms right above the solitary cells in Pavilion F, which means some are sleeping two to a bed and others on makeshift mattresses. On the other hand, it's useful having them where they are: it's easier dragging them down a floor to solitary than from all the way over in the other wing, especially since there are no elevators, so you have to bring them down the stairs, and sometimes my colleagues or I have to call for help, since the clients bite and dig in their heels, and if they really get unmanageable, then we give them a shot of rysol.

The CPMWDC decried "the Movement's dictatorial practices," but we aren't concerned, given how much less support than us they have. Though a decade ago Manhood Watch was arguing that even if our ideas were appealing to some women, our "terrorist activities" thoroughly discredited us, they now have on their conscience not only low-blow personal attacks on women in the Movement's leadership, but, according to the media, several recent kidnappings of our ideologues, two of whom remain missing.

Changing out of my guard's uniform into my civvies, I realize that, viewed from the outside, my work might seem like a grind.

"You're sacrificing your best years to men like some country girl from the last century," my mother joked the last time she came to visit, and I shot back that it was only thanks to the work of people like me that the best years of a woman's life now were the ones just before she succumbed to the afflictions of old age, and given that at this point China is only churning out apparel for regions where the Movement has yet to take hold, our country has not only seen an upswing in birth rate for the first time in decades, but our textile factories have opened back up, so one of the reasons the Movement has resonated so strongly here is that besides creating a new basis for relationships it can also take credit for the creation of new jobs. When I explain it that way, though, it makes it sound so trite, I think to myself as I lie on my couch. I confess, I've been enjoying my free time more and more these days.

"You've sacrificed your own freedom for the sake of other women's," my mother wrote in an email a week ago that I still haven't answered yet. We're always poking each other like that. The life I'm living now makes total sense to me, and my mother knows it. My work here at the Institute gives my life a meaning I could never get from a husband and children in the countryside, and besides, I can get a pass to go see the kids whenever I want to.

The name we use for the children's treatment facilities is "Gardens," and there are only a few, since there aren't too many boys who still treat girls badly at this point. (Schools, apart from a few whose principals are still rebelling, have all implemented the Movement's teachings across the board.) Typically, boys are interned in parallel with their parents (who are legally responsible for them), and the girls we intern are generally the daughters of women from backwater towns, where the Old World still survives, almost like a museum piece.

It's just a matter of time before we have actual museums of the Old World, complete with interactive videos about plastic surgery clinics and women's beauty contests, and spotlighted displays like in a museum of medieval torture, only with cosmetics and fashion magazines instead of torture instruments—a guaranteed draw. Museums as a deterrent, warning visitors not to forget the way it was, so those days will never be repeated. I picture my clients' sons and daughters walking through the exhibits, discussing long-defunct practices like women shaving their armpits and plucking their eyebrows, while a clip from an old radio broadcast crackles through the hall: "If the state continues to support the defilement of the natural relationship between men and women as cultural policy, smearing the traditional family model of minority communities and sending their members to camps, we will soon be facing nothing less than civil war ..." And as the voice of the Manhood Watch spokesman thunders from the fifteen-year-old recording, I practically burst out laughing. How long has it been since the last time there was talk of civil war? The term they used for what happened turned out to be something totally different. I count on my fingers, each year a milestone for the Movement. After Rita's apology for the terrorist attacks came the establishment of the first Community Center (proof that the enemy wasn't men but the Old World, which boosted the Movement's credibility on the skeptical outskirts of Europe); and it suddenly occurs to me I haven't put anything in my memoirs yet about the Movement's relationship to minorities, and the reason it occurs to me is that I can see out the window of my studio into the windows of Pavilion F, where the forest refugees are being housed, and though women in a sense were a minority in the Old World, the minorities coming into Europe at that time from more backward parts of the world tended to be hostile to the Movement's ideas.

Shortly after the attack on the plastic surgery clinic, Rita and the inner circle of Movement leaders received a group of Muslim women who she described as her "sisters in an exponentially more difficult situation."

The joint declaration issued a few days later spoke of a general "improvement of conditions." Rita took heat for the fact that the statement didn't actually bind anyone to do anything, but she made up for it shortly after with her now-renowned Solomonic proposal. Meanwhile Manhood Watch tried to dissuade the Muslim women from working with the Movement by pledging speedy processing of their immigration papers, while trying to claim that the joint declaration, titled "In Defense of the Interests of Non-European Women," opened the door to polygamy, in an attempt to spur the Old World men of Europe to rise up in another wave of resistance to the Movement (of course the statement didn't say a thing about polygamy, and Manhood Watch's legal advisers were well aware of that).

As I see the refugees across the way gesturing excitedly, I estimate that there are twice as many of them in each room as the hygienic standards of the Institute prescribe, and I am genuinely ashamed. Unfortunately, the alternative of "just leaving them be" to die out on their own was out of the question given their subversive activities, and every other Institute within driving distance of here was even fuller than ours (in a moment of premature euphoria, thinking the fight had been won, the Movement had recently allowed some of its smaller facilities to be privatized).

A fence was built, I write, and looking up again I see the refugees pounding on the windows. The whole time out there, holed up in the woods, they were running away from European values. From a purely statistical standpoint, there must have been at least a few Muslims among them.

A fence was built, I write, at the time of Rita's meeting with her "sisters in an exponentially more difficult situation." A fence dividing the largest refugee camp in Central Europe in half, separating the men from the women. The camp was on the grounds of a former international airport, repurposed several years earlier, and the Muslim men interned there objected that living without women was against the Qur'an, while the women complained that the men didn't know how to take care of themselves, citing the meals that wouldn't be cooked and the cleaning that wouldn't be done, causing the male part of the camp to descend into misery, filth, and chaos.

Rita shrewdly bundled the women's demand for the fence to be abolished in with her own proposal, so it didn't even take a visit from the camp administration, who in response to the protests against the fence just kept stubbornly repeating, "They're reproducing faster than our capacity permits," a message that became famous for its bureaucratic obtuseness, since capacity in itself doesn't permit anything. Except in this case, unfortunately, capacity wasn't even sufficient to provide the people in the camp with dignified living conditions, and the fence was the best idea the government could come up with (the World Health Organization flat-out forbade them from sterilizing the women).

I alternate between writing and rummaging through the documents that I've been bringing home over the past few weeks in order to have something factual to base my memoirs on. Because, despite their increasingly ridiculous agenda and shrinking number of sympathizers (their views are now so marginal that some of their members confess to them only in private), Manhood Watch is known for jumping on factual inconsistencies like a chicken on a worm, so I don't want to give them any openings. Especially since I have it all right here at my fingertips, and damn, where did I put that document with Rita's quote in it? I clearly remember downloading it and printing it out. You're a hopeless mess, I chide myself. Then I realize it's at the bottom of the pile.

"Women are eligible to reside in the men's section of the camp after menopause," says the quote in the document that unleashed a wave of heated debate, on social media as well as within the camp itself. The camp's young women launched a hunger strike, standing at the fence that separated the camp from the public (people would come give them food and toss used clothing and toys across), banging pots and pans. The women wore signs around their necks with messages in English like *I'm a year away from menopause and they still won't let me in*, *Let me rejoin my husband*, and *No discrimination on the basis of fertility,* while Rita gave interviews to TV stations from around the world, explaining her motives over and over again. In any case, Rita's proposal was the only compromise the camp administrators were willing to accept.

"The proposed measure addresses the absence of women without introducing the risk of further reproduction by the residents," the official in charge of the camp declared. His name was dragged through the mud as a fascist, and even some members of the Movement disagreed with the measure, stating, "We reject unfreedom as a means of liberation for minorities." But the biggest problem was the men affected by the measure. If the proposal was meant as a litmus test (or, if you will, Rita's Trojan horse), it worked, because the men protested that they didn't want the women after menopause. At that point it became clear that the debate was just the tip of the iceberg, and it wasn't about the breaking up of families or devoted couples who could only wave through the fence to each other, but the men's aversion to women who didn't get their periods, even though there was nothing about it in the Qur'an. So most of the women who qualified to move to the male part of the camp returned to the women's half voluntarily after a few days (the TV stations filmed their tears, but they refused to speak), and the refugees' relationship with Rita, and by extension with the Movement as a whole, from that point on could be described as lukewarm at best.

The Movement continued to recruit intensively among Muslim women, but even with the help of interpreters most of them "weren't able to grasp the basic ideas," I write, well aware that Manhood Watch will attempt to exploit my candidness by labeling me a xenophobe. But in accordance with the principles of the Movement, I look out at the world from myself, not at myself through the eyes of the world, those paralyzing lenses of obedience and self-censorship. There's no other way to think critically, whatever risk of attack it may bring. Without critical thinking, the Movement wouldn't be the Movement. We've never been interested in being a political party.

So what was the Muslim women's response?

That, too, was a milestone: When people hear the phrase "burka action" nowadays, they probably picture the conflicts at European universities from way back when, or the protests at the Olympic Games in Pyongyang a few years later, when the women's hurdles competitors insisted on their "uniforms." But when we say "burka action" what we're referring to is the reaction of Muslim feminists to Rita's "impromptu" statement (as the critics like to call it), meaning their open letter to Rita recommending ("in accordance with the intentions of your worldview") the "veiling" of everything female as a universal solution to the problems in society the Movement was struggling with. Conceal the female body under fabric ("as a shield against Satan's temptation," they said), and our troubles will be over. In a way, the tracksuits we wear now are an acknowledgement of that, as well as proof of our lack of cultural prejudice.

For a moment, I regret not having a mirror in my studio. If I wasn't holding the blanket in place with my hands, there wouldn't be anything to see of me but my eyes—but I am, so my bare arms are sticking out as well. I squeeze my elbows against my body to keep the blanket from sliding off and hop on two legs over to the window. Like a potato sack race in a life that isn't mine at all, because my mother was right, everything from my past has drifted away from me now, like it was never even mine: relatives, schools, my childhood room, their place in time swaying backward and forward like a rocking horse (was my first day of school before I had chicken pox, or after?). And it isn't only my childhood, but my teens and adult years, up until the bus came to a stop at that curve in the road and I climbed out with that awful wheeled suitcase of my mother's and the jagged silhouette of the meatpacking plant appeared, shimmering in the hot air like a desert oasis. Everything that happened before I got my first assignment (selling promotional materials in the little shop in the ground-floor lobby to the left of the fountain), I left all of that behind, outside the walls, and I rarely remember it anymore.

Since I don't have a mirror, I stare at the window (if I focus on the glass just right, it works fine as a mirror), breathing into the blanket wrapped around me, and I imagine myself as a woman of Islam, hiding my body from Satan's confederates to rid men of temptation, and it's every bit as Old World as stiletto heels and flawless makeup, this kowtowing to the so-called animal nature of so-called men, playing the snake in the grass of gender, singing to charm the cobra, lulling men into a state of obedience. The concealment of a woman's exterior only places it on a pedestal, while her insides are mainly used to manipulate her outsides: to care for her looks so they either glow with youth or don't exist at all. Unlike burkas, our tracksuits don't hide a woman's shape. The only essential thing that they conceal is the human soul.

I must have leaned too far forward, as my forehead bumps against the glass and I open my eyes with a start. All at once it's like a curtain has lifted, revealing the scene of the refugees' faces, men's faces, pressed against the glass of the windows across the way, gaping at me (I wonder how long they've been watching), and if I'd been in a bra, I would have thought they were spying on me, but

I'm wrapped in a blanket and the look in their eyes isn't that of lust, but of incredulous amusement. I know that look from the faces of the men the patrol vans bring here from places where people have barely heard of the Movement (as well as small patches of territory that nurture lasting resistance right in our backyard) when we check them in and confiscate their underwear, then hand them a two-page comic-strip card like the ones they have on airplanes that show you what to do in case of an emergency. The expression on the face of the masturbating man in the fourth panel is like the one on the man who shows you how to put on your oxygen mask: that same impassive coolness—one just before death, the other just before climax, but both watching the same TV melodrama—and the card for new clients is laminated, not so it's easy to clean off the cum, like the albums of labia photographs, but because we have only a few of them, for cost-saving purposes, so we always request that new clients, who need to learn the rules, not bring the cards back with them to their rooms, but leave them behind for the next clients who come along.

I wave to them. The faces crowded into the windows of the makeshift dormitories across the way. I wave to our newest clients, and on their faces I read: Someday we'll make you pay for our time here at the Institute. To which I respond in my mind: You've already had to give up your underwear, and our procedures were only vaguely explained to you when you arrived, so you're afraid of what will come next.

Fear of the unknown is often the main thing we're up against. Fear of making the discursive leap that we demand of them and completely remaking their way of seeing the world. Fear of letting go of the rope and trusting the Institute as they fall (a process involving the serious psychotic states that accompany any true transformation of the mind).

A guard walks in to check up on the clients across the yard. Squinting hard, I recognize her as she gives the men a dressing-down (apparently over the mess they've made in their lockers).

There were apples in their snack packs and they tossed the cores on the beds, I deduce.

That and, instead of being neatly stacked on the shelves, their clothes are crumpled in balls on top of the sheets, assuming they even made their beds. Meanwhile the laundry will have been running nonstop to make sure they all have clean bedclothes. But arguing with men who have it fixed in their heads that we're doing them an injustice is a waste of time, and my colleague knows that. Having chewed them out, I can see her handing out instructional materials with a smile.

Prior to reeducation, any clients with a history of resistance that isn't only private but ideologically organized (the last bunch we took in had attacked several women's communities in the area: slitting chickens' throats, trampling crops, even raping the women themselves) are required to undergo quarantine, followed by an individualized course of study before being introduced to the standard procedures (they're all addled in the brain, but each in a different way). This priority care is a sort of positive discrimination that enables clients with a history of armed resistance and mass violence to start from the same place as everyone else. It helps them overcome their lag in education, much like the special care devoted to Romani children before they enter elementary school to compensate for any neglect in their upbringing.

I write, watching the time to make sure I don't miss the start of my shift and catching occasional snippets from the radio. A listener calls in to complain (from the sound of their voice a man from my mother's generation) of having difficulty telling people apart. Walking down the street, he says hello to total strangers but walks right by his own family members without even noticing. He describes going to meet his daughter at the movies and circling the crowd in front of the theater, mortified.

"I couldn't even recognize my own daughter!"

I consider calling the station to ask for his personal contact details. We offer outpatient services in Institutes near a person's place of residence, and if necessary, we could send a van out to pick up the man. But I fully agree with the program's host that these are problems everyone faces and there's really nothing wrong. It's like complaining you can't fly or wishing you had night vision. Instead of lamenting the state of society, he should get a new glasses prescription, or ask his daughter to wear a less common color of tracksuit and decorate the hood, just to be safe.

I throw on my uniform—about time. The heads of the clients in the windows of the block opposite are gone. Apparently my colleague ordered an earlier lights-out because of the ruckus. A few of them are probably strapped down to their beds. On the way to see my clients, I run into a group of men huddled suspiciously in the hallway by the toilets. As soon as they catch sight of me, they all lower their eyes. I check their IDs: registration number, phase of reeducation, assigned guard, section head. What the hell are they doing here just before lights-out?

"Breathe on me," I tell the lanky man on the edge of the bunch (fortunately there's no alcohol involved). "You haven't brushed your teeth."

"I can't fall asleep," he says before launching into some nonsense about a chilled bladder and how they were squatting out in the garden picking zucchini well into the cold, late hours of the night. Underneath his words, I clearly detect a reproach for the fact that they aren't allowed to wear underwear.

"Empty your pockets," I command, and when that turns up nothing, I add, "Open your sweatshirts and drop your pants."

The man on the far right shakes with rage as photos of naked girls the age of their daughters fall to the ground, pinned inside the men's baggy pants. They must have stolen the safety pins from their sewing circle (I'll report it to the section head; whoever was overseeing them will be punished for her negligence). Lucky for them they're just at the start of their treatment, when we're still lenient toward breaches of discipline (at this point they know the right things to say, but haven't yet internalized the Movement's ideals).

"It's solitary for you, friends," I announce. Maybe while they're locked up alone they can finally get a grip on themselves and stop being such a disgrace.

I flag down two novices walking along the hall, each carrying two dummy torsos to a classroom for the morning workshop the next day.

"Escort these four clients here to the cooler in F," I say, using the slang from the old meat-packing plant. "Tell the section head we got some smut on A level two."

"What smut? Just a couple of pictures," the lanky man objects. His buddy next to him laughs. I should just lock the both of them up and throw away the key for being insubordinate. Instead I decide to take them with me.

"Follow me," I order, and as we pass the door to my office, I bark at them to take a seat in the hallway till I return.

I dash over to my clients in the rear wing on the second floor of Pavilion B, arriving just as the lights are going out, one by one. They've been waiting for me to make my evening rounds, but they know sometimes I get held up by my duties, and in case that happens the dormitory leaders have clear instructions to turn out the lights themselves. If there's anything urgent I need to discuss with one of my clients, I can always pull them out into the hallway later and make my rounds with a flashlight. Personally I'm responsible for three rooms, meaning I'll be terminated if anyone in them slits their wrists (part of my job is making sure they don't have anything to do it with), and I'm the first person they turn to with any requests. The following details concern "my" clients only, because they're exemplary. And to ensure the men's identities aren't exposed even after the fact, in the Institute annals, the names I use here are fictitious, as are their room numbers.

In number eight, the client who sleeps by the door is missing. He suffers from bulimia and vomits before lights-out on a regular basis. "Punishes himself with self-loathing for atrocities committed against his wife," his file says.

As I make my inspection, he walks back into the room from the toilets, looking pale and weak. "Wash your hands and into bed!"

I ask if he plans to masturbate before going to sleep, and offer to plot it out on a chart to give him immediate feedback, but he shakes his head no. He pulls from his pocket a carved figurine of Rita, the size of the Venus of Dolní Věstonice, though it looks more like a horse.

Woodworking is one way that clients here pass the time. There are those who do it because they enjoy it and those who do it for money: the men who use tobacco or porn barter for it with the products they make, and the men who want to send something home to their families (as a gesture of goodwill for having screwed up), sell their woodworking projects (assuming they have an appropriate ideological theme) for a small sum in the ground-floor gift shop.

As I look at Libor lying on the bed, I remember the closing of his letter to his mother, *Your beloved Libor.* You never would have guessed this scrawny man had a respectable career in banking while working in printed circuit boards on the side, and whenever I hear of anything that smacks of old technology, the thought of Pornjoy immediately comes to mind and my stomach flips.

I realize I'm holding the wooden horse—apparently Libor handed it to me, and now he's asking me my opinion about art. We have plenty of educated clients who can speak at length on the subject, especially if it allows them to avoid tougher issues, closer to home. But what is art about if not the art of living? We've already abolished fashion, and except for men of my mother's generation, like the one I heard on the radio, whose problem could be completely and easily solved by a stronger pair of glasses or some decorative flair on his daughter's tracksuit, most people are grateful for the end of fashion trends. In fact, it occurs to me, tracksuits are as timeless as caftans, and while Libor would have looked like a skeleton in the bankers' uniform of a three-piece suit, the hundred percent cotton of the tracksuit helps to soften his shoulders' hard edges. Though I feel sorry for him, his bulimia is a manifestation of his bad conscience (even after his wife had been through several plastic surgeries, he still wasn't satisfied, and in one illegal clinic, operated out of somebody's basement, she even caught a fungal infection).

"Why does this figurine of Rita look like a horse?" I ask without answering his question. The fact that I'm ignoring it is an answer in itself.

Libor just shrugs.

"Your request for release was denied."

He curls up under the covers like an animal. His wife doesn't want to see him, at least not yet, and the attending physician gave the standard reason for rejecting his mother's request that he be discharged: "High probability of recidivism."

Libor doesn't ask for details, just grabs the horse away from me and slips it back under his pillow. The typical wounded ego, I think, and make a mental note to instruct the morning shift to make sure Libor gets something for breakfast tomorrow that he won't immediately vomit back up. Then I pull the letter from his mother out of my pocket. After a long spell of silence, she finally wrote a reply, and apart from one term of abuse directed at the Institute, we didn't have to censor it at all. Libor's whole face lights up as he tears open the envelope and devours the letter. But with each line he reads, his expression turns increasingly despondent. Apparently, his mother is on our side. An elderly lady for whom her son's well-being matters even more than her own (Libor used to run her errands for her every day), she urges him not to put a rash end to his treatment.

"At least once more in my life, I'd like to see you truly happy"—I see tears in his eyes, so I assume he's reading the part where his mother reminisces about the trip she took with him and his wife, Felicie, to the medieval fort of Levý Hradec, and I wonder if this man will ever be ... honestly, some things are just impossible to predict.

"Any comments on your treatment?" I ask Libor, who has wrapped himself up in the blanket again. He furiously shakes his head, like he did the first time, when I asked about masturbation. He's obviously exhausted from all the vomiting.

I wake Richard, in his bed beneath the window, by tugging on his blanket. He opens his eyes and sits up as if on command. He steps into his slippers and shuffles to the door. Out in the hallway, I ask him straight to his face how he can explain the reports I've had from the instructor in New World ethics that several times last week he refused to take part in class. As we stand facing each other, I ask him to take a seat on the bench, but he either ignores me or doesn't hear. In his eyes I see the defiant look of an Old World man, the type of defiance we break on the wheel. The last time I saw that look was on the face of a client who tried to escape over the fence during gardening class, his eyes bulging as they took his sizzled body down from the wires.

"What's this about?" I ask.

"You're trying to force me to abandon myself."

"It's a transitional stage in personality change."

"You want to strip us of our innermost essence."

The Institute is equipped with alarms we can pull in case we need "urgent assistance"—not only in the event of a physical confrontation, where the client is out of control, but also in the case of explosive emotions or overaggressive arguments. There are at least two devices in every hallway, as I subconciously reassure myself with a glance.

"There will be nothing left of me," Richard goes on, staring at the linoleum on the floor, and in that moment the smears I see there, left behind from someone's careless mopping, only add to the wave of anger I feel that everything here just keeps going in circles.

"You despise us," Richard says.

"Say that one more time, please, and look me in the eye. You'll see nothing there but the desire for a just world."

As I say it, I realize how long it's been since I spoke to anyone so personally. The last time was over the phone with my mother, when she criticized me for not paying enough attention to her (I replied that the only reason she was even in that luxurious retirement home was because of my work for the Movement—which I felt bad about, but she forced me into it).

"You aren't the first person to feel dejected," I tell Richard, "and you won't be the last."

"I'll never be the person I used to be again."

"What did you expect? If a cosmetic change was all it took, we would do it in outpatient facilities with regular doctors and invest the money it takes to operate the Institutes somewhere else."

In my eyes there is nothing but the desire for a just world. Whereas his shine with a yearning for the "good old days."

"You can't just stigmatize people's gender," Richard says.

Maybe he expects me to say, "It depends on which phase of reeducation you're talking about," but instead I order him to take off his pants, and he pulls them down precisely the way the Institute has trained him to.

In the dim night lights of the hallway, his penis stands out from the jet-black tangle of hair between his legs (a proposal from some of the guards that clients shave their genitals to allow closer monitoring has failed to pass the assembly several times now). I take hold of his penis, that sophisticated product of evolution, and nestle his balls in the palm of my hand like a kitten.

"He at least is one hundred percent on our side," I say, weighing Richard's member in my hand. It doesn't show the slightest change in size, and he doesn't have erectile dysfunction, I checked.

"A model specimen, and you want to go and ruin everything for him? The reason you don't get any letters from your wife isn't because she doesn't miss you. But we're going to keep the block in place until you stop with these sadomasochistic interpretations of yours."

It would be natural for me to be angry, but I want to give Richard a chance (the section head once warned me that I was "too tolerant").

He objects in a voice that seems to come from his belly: "The idea that my wife ordered me to be picked up on my way home from work like I was some stray mutt, then carted away in a paddy wagon and locked up here, is a downright fraud. My wife never requested any such thing."

"You only know what she tells you, whereas we know what's in both of your best interests," I say, and before he has a chance to reply (I see him taking a breath to launch a cannonade in response), I add: "What's in your wife's and your own personal best interest is the systematic sorting of visual information, on a totally unconscious, automated level."

I take his sleeping member in both hands and give it a gentle kiss.

"You see? No reaction whatsoever. He's farther along than you are. You should follow his example. We want to liberate you."

"You want to make us impotent."

I took reactions like that as an insult when I was a novice. I would find some excuse and go running back to my section head in tears. But now? My gaze wanders over to the alarm for a moment, but I quickly bring it back to the penis in front of me. It's him who needs help, not me.

"You all like to talk about freedom, but the second I lust for anyone other than the old lady on the poster over my bed, I get tased."

"What about your masturbating during workshops?" I say, thinking how few men realize their sex drive is a cage, and I don't know who's trying to help them get free of it besides us.

"Privilege isn't something you're entitled to by nature," I say, and unlike Richard, what I have in mind isn't women but the clients to whom I promised a field trip to the female torso factory as a reward for good behavior, and then I hear him utter the words, "We're going to end up extinct."

"Clearly you aren't aware, but the birth rate has gone up substantially over the last decade. Extinction isn't an issue."

"But that isn't us anymore," he says, and just then the alarm sounds.

I run off to respond to the emergency.

No doubt they think I'm snoring away in my office after making my rounds, I think as I sprint down the hall in the direction of the beeps.

I arrive to find the dorm-room door thrown open, the guards leading the sleepy-eyed clients out into the hall. Where will they put them, I wonder, with the Institute nearly full? (My smoking buddy says even the stalls down in the basement, where they used to store dog food made from chicken feet back in the meatpacking days, are full.)

Hanging from a hook that probably used to hold the window blinds in place is client three-oh-eight. It was only a few days ago that he shot his sperm into my glove.

The guard in charge of the room sits on the ground weeping while two others take care of the client (one cuts through the rope while the other holds him up with her hands on his behind). As the clients shuffle off down the hall, escorted by the guards, I hear a hot-tempered section head letting loose a string of curses.

"In the name of Rita, the Movement, and the Institute," I say, crossing myself the way we did when they pulled the scorched escapee down from the wires. Unlike him, this man has the look of a thinker. Like he fell asleep in the middle of solving some complex riddle, and if the question was what it would be like when he got out, he should have just asked one of the staff. From all indications, he couldn't cope with not being accepted to take the final exam. I notice the black circles under his eyes as I help my colleagues lower the corpse to the ground, next to his suitcase. He was so sure he was leaving, he had already packed. The sheet was still tied around his neck. An unstable client who failed to pass the penis stimulation test and lacked adequate supervision. Part of what makes this so awful is that I was present for his debacle last Monday. Crumpling the sheet with one hand in his sleep, his leg poking oddly out from under the blanket, he came so hard he groaned like he was giving up the ghost. As it turned out, his last gasp was still yet to come.

I wrap my arm around my sobbing colleague's shoulders. I don't know her by name, but I can tell from her uniform she hasn't been working here long, and the paleness of her face makes it plain that she's in shock.

"First time for you, huh?"

"Poor Jiří, poor Jiří" are the only words she can muster. It's typical for novices to have a stronger bond with clients, and my memoirs aren't a tell-all so I won't go into detail about what it's like when a novice falls for one of the men and then it isn't just the porno mafia hanging around the toilets but Institute staff getting intimate with clients as well. Undeniable evidence of failure on both sides, documented by cameras. Their punishments are broadcast over the PA.

As two of my colleagues lift the body and carry it away, the guard on whose watch the death occurred recovers enough to get back on her feet and resume her duties. The first task is filling out the forms for Jiří's file. Then the section head will complete it with a final report and deposit the file in the archive.

"Can I help?" I ask. "A client of mine died of diabetes recently."

I give the guard a hug, then help her complete the paperwork. Before I leave, I take one last look around the empty room. I notice they need new light bulbs. Two of the three are broken. Self-criticism shouldn't mean the clients have to ruin their eyes. While I try to work out which section head the room falls under so I can submit the request for new lights (one less thing for my shaken colleague to do), I walk my fellow guard back out to the hall and lock the door. She can come and recover in my office.

As I drag her along behind me, I wonder whether I should offer her some rysol. I keep a few doses in my office just in case. (When my client died, I gave myself a shot twice, for my nerves; lucky for me, the only one who got fired for it was the doctor who wrote me the prescription.)

Meanwhile I had totally forgotten about the two men I instructed to wait for me outside my office. They were still there on the bench in the hallway when I returned, one slumped over the other, fast asleep.

As my colleague and I enter my office, she wearily asks for a glass of water, then tells me to go ahead and see to my duties. I lay her on the couch and tuck her under a blanket, then invite the clients in. They shuffle through the door. With my colleague under the blanket, it looks like it's just me, the two of them, and a lumpy mess stuffed under the covers on the couch. The questioning can begin. I take down the men's registration numbers and open their files. Sons of good families, spoiled brats aware enough to know what the consequences of their behavior are.

"How far along are you in your reeducation?"

They start in again with the same stupid smirks as their buddies back at the toilets. Back there they acted tough. Not anymore. Not when their lives are at stake. These two were transferred here from the Gardens as teenagers, to complete their treatment, so in light of their age and the fact that their families have always willingly cooperated with the Institute, I decide to drag their parents into it.

"All it takes is one phone call," I say, "and your mothers' high-ranking positions will be in serious trouble."

"I'm responsible for myself," declares one man with confidence. I take down his response. This is just a preliminary investigation before I hand the matter over to my section head.

"What would your mother say if she knew what you were doing with your sperm? In an institute she pays for with her taxes. Do you have any questions about your curriculum?"

My colleague on the couch shifts beneath the blanket, and the two clients shake their heads in unison.

"Is there something you don't understand? Do you not like it here?"

These two are typical, saying OK to everything even though it means nothing to them. Carrot-and-stick is the only approach that works with clients like them—solitary being the standard stick for pornographic magazines and visits being the motivational carrot that we ban for any client who refuses to cooperate.

The main question now, though, is whether these two were just looking at porn or if they're actually part of the mafia.

Their eyes dart around the room before landing on the line of Rita busts that I keep in my display case (the asbestos one on the end comes from my colleagues who attended the anniversary celebrations).

I formulate my question and take aim. "If you don't have any questions about the curriculum, how do you explain the fact that you had prohibited materials in your pants?"

A moan comes from the couch, followed by a deep sigh, and the clients exchange a look of surprise. (I only slipped a single teaspoon of rysol into my colleague's glass of water.)

"I told you we should have reported it immediately," client two-twenty-two says to his partner.

"The whole reason we got together was to burn it," says client eight-one-five, and the first one adds, "Tom found it over there in—"

I slam my fist down as hard as I can. But the only impact it has is on my desk. The clients go on snooping around my office with their eyes, as if the refurbished furniture from the days of the meatpacking plant (the only new piece is my ergonomic chair) offered a boost to their self-confidence.

"Tom found it in the bushes there," blurts

client eight-one-five. "In the bushes over by the horses, out in the yard," and now I know they're porno mafia, because the bushes by the horses is the mafia's meeting place; they leave the materials in a box of vegetable shortening in exchange for money or a favor in return. And the reason I know is a woman from the maintenance crew stumbled across a drop-off there while cleaning the yard a few days ago. The porno mafia tried to discredit her by claiming she was the connection, but our staff had been keeping their eyes on the spot (pretending to be clients raking leaves), so there was no way anyone could have found anything there in the interim.

"So how did he know?"

"He didn't. He was just walking by and stopped to take a leak."

On any other day, I would have blown my top and pointed out that that's why we have toilets on the ground floor, but right now I have a higher purpose than hygiene.

"Why would he dig around in the branches to go pee?"

"How should I know?" shrugged two-twenty-two. "But it wasn't in the branches, it was lying on the ground, just behind the leaves around the edge."

"Just lying out in the bushes?" I can't resist a snide comment as I see the snare hanging over them like the clouds above the meat-packing plant when the rain blows in from town. I pull it tight like the cord on the drawstring bag I used to carry with me to school in the days of my youth; or like the ones on the old women's torsos they ship to us from the factory, which come in fabric drawstring bags (from places these two will never go to on a field trip as a reward), because before they started shipping them in bags, the torsos used to arrive at the Institute all beat-up like I am now from living a life of service.

And two-twenty-two says, "Yeah. The pictures were just lying there on the ground, so he picked them up."

"Nothing wrong with that, is there?" says eight-one-five, in a desperate attempt to regain the upper hand.

They claim they were going to report the find and turn in the materials, so I ask them point-blank whether their prestigious families (mothers in managerial jobs, fathers lecturing on gender theory and actively involved in their sons' education) smuggled the filth in to them on a visit, or whether they were trafficking in the pictures for financial gain or some other quid pro quo.

They glance right, then left. The noose of accusation is wrapped around their necks, and they have no alibi. There is a raspy snore from the couch, then the room falls silent.

"Even with the workshops, I just can't help it," eight-one-five finally blurts. "I know what the Movement's trying to do, and I'm sympathetic to its goals, but I am what I am."

He throws up his hands just as the guard on the couch rolls over onto her other side. Soon she'll wake up, and the fourth case of suicide in the past six months will land on the section head's desk.

"Lots of guys just cheat their way through this whole thing," two-twenty-two adds defiantly.

For his tone alone, he deserves at least half on top of whatever punishment he gets for the porn. It's the ones from privileged families with a good profile whose bodies deceive them most often, I think, making a note to myself: "Check ideological background on families of two-twenty-two and eight-one-five."

Mostly, though, I'm thinking about the next thing I want to say, which is: "You can't cheat your way into the final exam."

If they see the Institute as unsatisfactory in some respects, so be it, but one thing we're definitely not is obtuse.

"After solitary, it's back to the albums again for you," I say. Then, following my boss's example, I attempt a mixture of warmth and strictness: "Maybe the second time around, you'll come to your senses, and if not ..." I offer an enigmatic expression. To make sure they picture our famous electroshock helmets—the ones my colleagues' children play with in the Institute nursery school after the helmets are taken out of circulation—I draw a halo around my head with my hands (with my fingers as the feelers). That alone is enough to make both clients flinch.

"Out!" I scream.

The two novices waiting in the hallway immediately take charge of the men, escorting them off to solitary as per my instructions.

"He's going straight to heaven" are the first words I hear out of my colleague's mouth as she throws off her blanket. But who knows? She's mumbling pretty badly, and I've been on duty for twenty hours nonstop, so I'm not exactly fresh. She looks older than she did a few hours ago. My colleague was one of those people who joined the Institute later in life, which tends to happen when somebody hits a bump in the road. She was missing a few teeth, both above and below.

"So did you and Jiří have a relationship?" I ask.

It wouldn't be the first time, or the last, and the Institute regulations make no mention of it, but by unspoken agreement it's up to the section heads' discretion. They generously overlook certain infringements and extenuating circumstances, one of which is: older women lacking in Old World appeal.

"We engaged in practical training together." She loudly blows her nose.

"Nothing beyond Phase Six," she adds,

looking me straight in the eye. I almost can't even see hers through her thick, droopy eyelids. The skin on her cheeks sags, collecting along her jaw, and apart from the shadow of a mustache beneath her nose, common in women of her age, whiskers dot her chin and her eyebrows are fused in the middle. She wrings her hands, almost as if squeezing out her confession: I'm waiting for the gory details and she knows it.

"The woman on Jiří's poster was at least five years younger than me," she says, pulling the rolled-up poster from the leg of her giant sweatpants.

I take my glasses from my desk drawer and study the pattern of stretchmarks on the model's belly. The skin is so loose it covers most of her pubic area. Only a small tuft of gray curls is visible.

"He also chose a woman with a disability several times," my colleague says, blowing her nose again.

"Of course, we always stopped when they took down the posters before the final exam," she adds firmly in response to the question she must have been expecting.

If this weren't just a private conversation between the two of us, but an interview with her section head, and the mic in my office weren't covered with duct tape, that answer alone would have settled the matter from a judicial point of view. Because while the goal in Phase One is to dissolve the Old World association between male arousal and a young woman's body, aided in part by clients' compulsory masturbation while viewing posters of mature models, once that has been achieved the goal is to eliminate completely the association between arousal and an inanimate body the client feels no personal connection to.

"So, before the final exam there was no further contact between you?"

She shakes her head side to side like a little girl. The few gray wisps that remain of her once-probably-blonde hair don't even move, flattened against her head by the baseball cap that's part of our guard's uniform. (Some of my colleagues only take them off in their office.)

I could just as well have said, "So you didn't sleep together after that?" but we hardly know each other (only in passing, from the canteen), so I address my colleague in official Institute language and she responds in kind: "Mostly I would go and see him on my lunch break, and later he would come see me in my office, sometimes at night too, during consultation hours. First we would look through the albums of old women I use in the workshop. He always wanted to masturbate to the one in the middle with the missing teeth." She laughs uneasily.

"So that's why you let him knock them out?" I say, pointing to her mouth as I offer her sugar for her coffee.

"When he was coming to see me, I wouldn't brush my teeth for several days, and just before we met, I would eat a whole clove of garlic."

"Did the section head know about this?"

My colleague gazes absently out the window.

They'll be coming for morning wake-up soon, I realize, looking across the way in the same direction as her. The clients will start a new day, the section heads will announce the latest news and the daily schedule over the

PA, and Jiří will be buried in the cemetery.

The plot is only a quarter full. You can see its western corner from the canteen, and with binoculars, the tips of the individual tombstones are visible even from here, bearing the names of the men laid to rest there in urns.

"I would breathe the garlic in his face while he masturbated. The idea was to enhance the experience as he went into the next phase of the workshop—with the permission of the section head of course. I never got the chance."

My colleague's voice breaks as her eyes fill with tears.

"That's easily rectified," I say, trying to console her.

She shoots me a look.

"Can you bring him back to life?"

Ashamed, I give no reply.

"When I passed out from hyperventilating, he revived me with a French kiss. Stuck his tongue right in there, garlic and all. Sometimes I would eat ripe cheese or a can of pickled herring before he came to see me."

She pauses a moment, closing her eyes.

"He covered my face with kisses, and then when I accidentally belched, flooding the office with garlic, he said, 'I love you,' and came on the spot. I totally lost my head. You might object that that was from fainting—of course—but it's a proven fact that love can cause a physiological deficit."

My colleague seemed to be looking out through the window and through the building across from us, into her own inner landscape.

"Jiří fell in love with me regardless of my body and the odors it was giving off, and it wasn't just garlic and fish and ripe cheese. I never, ever, ever showered before our consultations."

She shrieks in agony, then bursts into tears again.

I hand her a handkerchief. She honks into it with gusto, her face red as a you-know-what in heat, I think inappropriately, and it occurs to me that in the moment when Jiří declared his love for her, he couldn't have been any further from that, any further from animalism and closer to the humanity of a penis with an IQ of 130, as we describe the transformation that men here undergo to visitors to the Institute. Whether it's rysol or electroshock that does the trick, eventually my colleague will forget the whole thing, like everything unpleasant that comes with a fundamental change for the better.

"I would say you did the best you could to prepare Jiří for the final exam," I hear myself tell my colleague, and now my eyes are welling up, too. "So why do you think he made such a mess of the entrance exam? There's no doubt that he ejaculated, and the procedure I performed was absolutely standard. You can verify that in his file for yourself."

I look into my mug, feeling uneasy that my colleague might think I blame her for Jiří's death, which is the last thing I would want. When a client can't come to terms with a setback, despite the many opportunities they have to attempt to address it, the responsibility lies entirely with them, and my colleague more than made it up to the Institute for overstepping her authority, by rendering services far beyond the scope of her duties.

As I raise my eyes, I'm startled to see her standing in the window with her back to me.

Then I realize it's just her reflection and she's actually standing at my display case of Rita souvenirs.

"Do you really believe in all that?" she asks.

2

There are several reasons I'm making a trip to the women's Community Center. First, because the Movement explicitly recommends that Institute employees make regular visits to Institutes in other regions and affiliated Community Centers and Gardens (if the right hand doesn't know what the left is doing, the legs will get them nowhere, as we like to say). Second, I'm overworked, and there's nothing better for that than a brief change of environment. And third, I want to revisit the situation with Libor's and Richard's wives. Technically I'm responsible only for my clients' reeducation, but any treatment their partners are undergoing falls under the purview of the Community Centers, and coordination of the reeducation process for the couple as a whole is a crucial factor in determining the outcome of their lives. Not to mention, I'm tired of constantly confiscating the correspondence between Richard and his wife.

I still have the same wheeled suitcase from my mother that I brought with me to the Institute almost twenty years ago. I had the pocket zippers repaired and lubricated the wheel that scraped with a bottle of oil I borrowed from the cafeteria cooks. They wish me a pleasant trip, giggling and snorting into their pizza-dough-coated hands. (Simple women with no great ambition, I didn't expect anything other than crude humor from them. Two of them even used to belong to Manhood Watch. Institutes that struggle with a shortage of personnel are willing to look the other way when it comes to hires who have no ideological influence on the clients.)

I pack only a few necessities. (As an Institute employee, I'm automatically issued a tracksuit at any affiliated facility.) I take Libor's and Richard's personal files—on paper, just to be safe—and slip them into my larger suitcase pocket, where, by the way, I also discovered an age-old comb of mine, at this point totally useless, given how short my hair is.

I pack, and in my head I'm already on the road, or at least on my way out the front gate to the parking lot, where a van sits ready and waiting (a decommissioned patrol van with an outmoded GPS and windows built in with a welding torch, courtesy of our technicians).

I pack, counting the months since I last went anywhere—everyone thinks the clients are locked up in here, but really we're the ones who don't set foot outside the place. It's a paradox of fate that the animals brought here for slaughter when it was still a meat-packing plant usually spent no more than a few hours here, whereas Institute staff are cooped up inside for years, despite our total freedom, and whenever a reason presents itself to go out in the world, some special occasion like the anniversary of Rita's speech in Europarliament, the people who take advantage of it are, to be blunt, usually the ones with the least scruples about missing work. And aren't they the ones who deserve a break the least? The ones whose conscience allows them to shirk their duties?

To be honest, my section head has been literally screaming at me for months to get out of here and take a break, so I'll "stop making slip-ups." There's no way she could know that the main thing keeping me here the past few weeks isn't the clients but my memoirs.

I'm a chronicler by necessity, because nobody else is going to do this work. My second, unpaid shift, which I sit down to for a couple minutes even now, with my suitcase fully packed and the handle sticking up in the air, ready to go (it won't fully retract and now it's too late to repair). I open up my latest volume, for the sixth and next-to-last phase. Or last. Depending how you look at it.

In Phase Six, the old women's torsos the clients masturbate to in Phase Five are replaced by a workshop involving actual coitus. The job title for the women who fill this position, if written by Manhood Watch, might say something like "high priestess of the Movement." We describe them more prosaically as "realies." Here in the classroom we have several prime specimens, and these women too, like the models we use for our practice albums and posters, are recruited out in the field. There's also an office where models can come and apply on their own. The requirements are that they be mature in appearance, with a flexible schedule and willingness to handle a high workload. At this point in their reeducation, our clients can successfully masturbate to the photos of the women dismissed by the Old World as old and ugly in our practice albums—they don't advance to Phase Six otherwise. In addition, the men can explain the misguided reasons why these bodies were considered inferior, and although not required, our best students can also cite the relevant passages from Rita's writings.

For this exercise, the clients are seated around the classroom as usual. I open Phase Six as I would any other, with a brief introduction summarizing the role of this stage in familiarizing the clients with New World praxis and the contents of the final exam. The instructional torsos produced by the Institute factory are skillfully rendered imitations, but they aren't living beings, and it is precisely that gap between a faithful copy of a being and the being itself that we focus on in Phase Six. The realie's body is the bridge that clients have to take to cross that gap into the New World, and every client must cross it alone. The instructor simply monitors their progress, egging them on, and talking the fainthearted out of their faintheartedness.

The classroom is a little bigger than in other phases, to accommodate the stalls with curtains in the back. The realies wait readied in the stalls in advance, sitting naked on chairs. Generally, coitus takes place standing up, since we don't have room for parallel rows of cots. Behind the curtain in each stall we make ample lubricant available, as well as a glass of water in case either one of the pair should get thirsty at any point. To the extent resources allow, we strive for maximum comfort.

As already noted, clients at this stage of reeducation have a full appreciation for the qualities of a mature body, and it's more than just something they've read in a manual. The theory has been fixed in their minds over a series of ejaculations, in workshops as well as in their free time, alone in the dorms with the models on their posters, so it may seem Phase Six is nothing more than a trivial formality. And it is. Assuming that's an accurate description of the difference between a photograph and reality. A realie is three-dimensional, which is precisely what causes a problem for clients. All those folds, wrinkles, and hanging flaps are flat when they're on the page, but these women are endowed with authentic sagging flesh, quivering under the fingers or drooping across the ribs, and often abounding in richly textured scars or swaths of eczema.

"First group behind the curtains," I call out after giving my introduction. The men strip down, and while some of them wait for my instructions, those less confident start to masturbate in advance. We tolerate this in the earlier stages of Phase Six, but eventually they learn to heed my instructions to wait with their hands on their knees, and if they can't manage that, then to put them behind their backs, old-school style. Only rarely do we stoop to using the baton.

At this point, with a few exceptions, the clients are incredibly well disciplined. This doesn't alter the fact that only a minority of them succeed in having intercourse with the realies on their first attempt, but we try to make it as easy as possible for them. In addition to lubricant and a glass of water, there's also a bucket in every stall, in case of nausea. The women are well trained enough that they don't take anything personally, and for that matter, they're paid for their professionalism.

In the event of nausea, they may stroke the client's shoulders, or, at their own discretion, even gently fondle his penis. If need be, they simply slide the bucket to the client with an understanding smile. A successful coitus preceded by vomiting is just one of many possible outcomes, so we're basically glad to see it. Any client who's willing to come to grips with himself on that level deserves our highest praise. And to my readers from more backward areas, who may doubt the appropriateness of practicing sexual intercourse in a setting resembling a polling booth, I pose the rhetorical question: Do you vote any differently because there's a line of people waiting outside the curtain behind you? In the event a client fails, I just encourage them to work harder.

The men line up to take their turn, one after the other, with three to five men waiting outside the curtain. In the course of a typical lesson, each client gets at least one, often two, and sometimes even three attempts (if more than one client is absent from the workshop for illness or some other reason). After their first time with a realie, the men talk through their experiences with one another. Over the course of the following workshops, there's less and less rehashing each time, and if on any given day the room is silent, I take it as a good sign that there's nothing left to talk about, the clients have Phase Six down pat, and during the break I allow myself a cigarette in my office, or with my smoking buddy in the kitchen. Phase Six is one of her favorite topics of conversation.

I end work on my memoirs for the moment with no great conclusion, interrupted by the van honking its horn. Nearly forgetting my suitcase, I dash out of my room at the last minute, sprinting down several flights of stairs and riding two freight elevators (in my haste I make the mistake of riding all the way down to the basement, then have to come back up). I then race across the yard to the gate, my wheeled suitcase hopping and skidding behind me (you look absolutely ridiculous, my smoking buddy must be thinking, watching the comedy out the window).

I climb on board at the last minute and plop down into the first seat in front, behind the driver. I want to make sure I can see everything at the same time as her, instead of having to wait for a secondhand view of the scenery only after everyone in the rows ahead of me has looked. I gladly forgo joining my colleagues in waving goodbye to the Institute through the tiny little rear window—you'd think we were never coming back—then all my thoughts are drowned out by the screech of wheels as the van pulls out of the parking lot.

On our way from the Institute to the nearest city bus stop, the one where I stood in the sweltering heat when I first arrived as an incoming novice, we pass several cars driven by women carrying future clients, most of them snoozing away in the back seat the same way they were that day back then. We give the women encouraging waves, and they nod back with a smile, a smile I would call, in the best tradition of the Institute and the Movement, conspiratorial, and as we enter the city my colleagues eagerly dig into their snack boxes: apples, open-face sandwiches, and a liter bottle of water from Rita's Spring (a stroke of marketing genius on the part of the company; the spring in fact has no connection with Rita whatsoever). I open the bottle and take a long sip, then turn and drink in the landscape flashing by my window. It's been a long time since I was on the outside.

"Even in the Old World we didn't have wrecks like this." I hear my colleague across the aisle complaining about the van, and of course we put most of the funds we get from our donors into expanding our reeducation programs, not wasting them on some stupid employee frills, and I count out loud the dorm rooms we still have with leaky ceilings, not to mention that we need a ramp for our clients with disabilities, and new sprinklers for the garden, and a new line of client footwear, and an upgrade of our PA, and all sorts of other things far more pressing than modernizing our vehicle fleet, especially since in our case the van isn't going to pick up a client but dropping us off at places where it doesn't really matter if there's any delay or not.

My colleague behind me jokes that she feels like she's on a field trip of nuns. I stifle the urge to make a biting comment about what that comparison reveals about her and instead accept the pair of binoculars being offered to me by one of my colleagues and take in the view outside my window, noting every detail, from the squeaky-clean sidewalks to the texture of the tracksuits on the men pushing children in strollers.

After thousands of years of unpaid women's work, we can now talk about the targeted redress of this historical imbalance (as you know, the principle of collective guilt was first removed, then reinstated into the established discourse). And although scientific studies have thus far reached only preliminary conclusions as to the reasons why the successful reeducation of men results in the popularization of paternal care, the connection is obvious, as I can see for myself right now: men walking with children, men shopping with children. Not only that but the number of children is greater than it was in the days of my youth, when people claimed that Europe was dying out.

Unfortunately our experience with the New World is difficult to communicate to the countries we call "developing." Reflecting on the essence of our project, I drift off into my own private world and don't even realize it till one of my colleagues shakes me out of my reverie. Next thing I know, I myself am shaking, the binoculars are soaked from my outburst of emotion, and I can't see squat anymore.

In short: the following descriptions of the New World, as seen from a window acetylene-torched into the side of an Institute patrol van, are meant solely for the informational purposes of people in countries where the Movement is still in its infancy or doesn't even exist yet (a possibility unimaginable to me and my fellow passengers). To this last sentence I attach a row of exclamation points.

I wipe the moisture off the binoculars with a handkerchief from my thoughtful colleague and bring the ancient device back into focus.

We pass through the outskirts of town on our way to the first facility on our itinerary, where a couple of us will be dropped off. Though tracksuits these days are sold in a wide range of colors, black and gray are predominant here. Clearly, most people in the area pay more attention to hood decorations.

I have to smile thinking back on the way people used to write about clothes. It wasn't just Manhood Watch who spoke of "the terror of uniformity" (what else would you expect from them?), but even so-called serious intellectuals. Utter nonsense, scraping the bottom of the barrel, yet even after the authors' deaths it lived on, on social media. An ideological witch hunt, fueled by stupidity and the fashion lobby allied with the textile industry.

Leaving the main road, we enter the grasslands of the Czech steppe, and as we pass an Institute factory the driver makes a point of drawing it to our attention. I refocus the binoculars (my colleague asks for them back, but I act like I don't hear, and since she doesn't raise her voice to a whine I can get away with it) and see a truck exiting the bowels of the factory loaded with finished torsos, to be packed up and shipped off to all the Institutes, a leggy heap of crotches delivered to each address. On any other day, it could easily be carting a load of boxed milk or smelly plastic for recycling, and all of a sudden my nose flashes back to the odor of Pornjoy and the mix of paints I used to coat the torsos with. The trip seems to be taking forever, and as I pan the binoculars like a camera, I'm comforted to think even Rita would give a whoop of joy to see the roadside billboards free of naked bodies.

At one historic moment (a lengthy moment, stretching across one or two election periods), it looked like women's nude bodies on billboards would be replaced by men's. The Movement's radical ideologues promoted the theory of compensation ("now companies get to use your wieners to sell theirs"), but after a few failed ad campaigns with posters featuring men's chests as champagne trays ("Have a nice night out with Bohemia Crystal"), the bulging boxer shorts of a well-endowed second-rate actor to lure students to an unnamed private university ("Reach the climax with us"), and the rounded derriere of a bodybuilder on a palm tree–lined beach to sell vacation getaways ("Plop right down wherever you like"), the concept was abandoned. It didn't help the companies' sales, and a subsequent series of legal actions put an end to the practice.

I use the binoculars to look around the van at my colleagues too, focusing in on their acne, their freckles, the orange-rind skin on their arms. The truth is it's silly to say women can't be enticed by pictures of naked men to buy useless crap because they're naturally more intelligent. The term "mental level" describes the same thing much more aptly, and the phrase "Mental level reflects the extent to which one is prone to a simpleminded visualization of the body" is dead on target. Because a body without a mind is just a sack of shit, and the main difference between one body and another is the degree of density.

I remember reading about how crowds of

old uneducated white males, to use the ugly vernacular of the Movement in those days, took to the streets chanting, "Down with the new Nazism!" while Manhood Watch egged them on, along with the majority of conservative intellectuals. Of course that's all in the past now, and I'm not sure why I'm feeling the need to reminisce, except that maybe every journey through space is in some ways also a journey with or against the flow of time, and *zoom*, we pass a billboard for the notorious mineral water with Rita's face on the label (Old World commerce is hanging on tooth and nail in the New World, unfortunately), and I think how profiting off the reputation of famous people ought to be banned, just like we did with images of naked female bodies, and now I'm boiling mad.

Everyone in the van is sweating. People whiz by in their fancy electric cars on either side, while we, the artists of change, travel in spartan conditions. Thanks to our Institute license plates, at least roadblocks and speed limits don't apply to us, so while ordinary traffic has to detour around a section of road where construction is under way on a new facility for genetic experimentation, the police wave us through along with an ambulance. The only work going on in the huge pit for the time being is archaeological, and the next stop on our journey is the parking lot of a leisure-time supermarket: some of the windows in the van won't open so we ask the driver to stop and let us throw away our apple cores.

Two of my colleagues get out to smoke, which makes me think of my mother. I'm contemplating whether or not to stop by her place on my way back to the Institute. I probably will; outside of her retirement home, I'm the only one she's got.

While our driver charges up the van, the first two women prepare to be dropped off in the nearby Garden. They're going there undercover on a sensitive mission to investigate an accusation of pedophilia and aren't allowed to share the details. I wonder sometimes if it's more acceptable to be abused by an individual or a system, or is it just that we have more tolerance for one than the other, the way it is for some people with addictive substances, and the first thing I regret forgetting to bring with me is rysol, since we're going to be on the road all of tomorrow night as well.

I lift my eyes to the sky. The airport traffic out here is nonstop. A continuous line of planes, at regular intervals, flying along the famous East–West corridor. The Institute stipulated that flights be diverted from the airspace directly overhead. Two terrorist attacks were more than enough. As their influence wanes the radical cells of Manhood Watch are taking a harder line, it occurs to me as I reboard the bus, and I'm not the only one. The few towns under their control are no longer letting in women at all. Richard is a sympathizer, no doubt in my mind, I think, pulling out the notebook I use to take notes for my memoirs (my knees will work just fine as a desk), and I drag my shoe across the floor, scraping off a wad of gum I picked up in the parking lot. Every public rest stop in Europe is the same.

Taking things in order, the next section of my memoirs will be devoted to a description of Phase Seven, in other words the final exam, and before I drift off to sleep, I remember a story my mother once told me about taking a train to the Tatras when she was still a little girl. She fell asleep in the middle of the woods and woke at dawn to the sight of nothing but mountain peaks all around. That's what the area where I'm heading looks like, too.

I wake to find half my colleagues gone. One of them left a bottle of water on her seat, so I finish it off. Besides investigating the accusations of pedophilia, the other reason for my colleagues' visit to the Garden was to propose some changes to the curriculum, which allegedly wasn't even up to a first-grade level (when it came to reeducation they had excellent results, but the boys interned there couldn't even solve a simple word problem). Although to judge from the way my colleagues were badmouthing their section head at the Institute the whole way, my guess is it was as much about getting away from her as anything else.

For breakfast we stop at a diner with leatherette booths, straight out of an Old World American film. I think about the accusations against the Movement that it was "destroying natural relations between the sexes" and what a couple having a "natural breakfast" must have looked like a few decades ago. (I pick a table next to a glass partition, which gives me a view both into the restaurant and out the window, where I can see the driver fiddling with our luggage.) Drinking soup for breakfast through a short thick straw probably wasn't the rage back then. Or was it?

Either way, I order eggs. The waiter checks my order with me not once but twice—respectfully, but still. Besides the elderly couple by the toilets, I'm the only one in the place having eggs. My colleagues glance around, looking mildly alarmed, and I suppose I look the same, which would also explain the waiter's hardness of hearing, a cover for his suspicion that we might be from Inspection. Which in a way we are. Two plainclothes officers from the inspector general's office are giving the side-eye to everyone but us (members of the Movement can easily identify one another even without a uniform), while checking the papers of two women in the corner of the restaurant, apparently on suspicion of wearing makeup. And if anyone wants to call the New World a police state, be my guest. Because if you think it's important to fight for your ideals but that conquered territory can be left unprotected to go up in flames, you're either a Manhood Watch supporter (consciously or not), a trueborn ignoramus, or from a developing country in the Old World.

The eggs are cold and the TV on the wall is tuned to an underwater reality show where the contestants live in bottle-green bathyscaphes. It may be boring but I find it absolutely delightful.

Some novices argue that the screenings we hold twice a month in the Institute auditorium, an assortment of current documentaries with an occasional sprinkling of lighter, more relaxing fare, are "biased." They say we show the world as the Movement would like it to be, while the reality outside our walls, "which we seldom venture out into," is "far more complex." Young people love to criticize and that's why we have them here, but I've never heard the novices speak that poignantly about the situation "outside the walls," so in what way exactly is the image of reality that we present distorted? And if what really bothers them is the series' old-fashioned title (*Window on the World*), why don't they just say so? The objections I hear during our conversations in the kitchen always boil down to things like "the camera work was static" or "the structure was too conventional," and my breakfast in the diner only confirms that even interactions here "outside the walls" are one hundred percent in accordance with the Movement manual, so where's the bias in that? People here are sitting straight and acting correctly, nobody making goo-goo eyes or looking down anyone's shirt, no shows of submission or manipulative hissy fits, and the fact that the waiter is probably trans only boosts the positive feeling I have, since under the New World regime, where everyone has their hair cut short and dresses in tracksuits, you can't easily tell, and anyway nobody cares, and one of the (many) reasons for that is that the good of the community comes first in the New World, and the realization of the individual flows from there. It's been proven now, many times, the other way around doesn't work.

Out of the corner of my eye I see the driver gesturing it's time for us to go, so I pick up my food to take with me. If it hadn't dawned on the waiter before, he must know we're from the Institute now, because we all clean up our cups and plates and stack them on the counter next to the coffee dispenser, obviously confused that there's no dirty-dishes window. At any rate, at least it's clear we're not with Inspection. The inspector general's novices would never make the rookie mistake of cleaning up after themselves.

The driver drops off another two of my colleagues at a crossroads ("Just go straight a ways, then hang a right," she says in a motherly tone), and they disappear down the dusty road, each with nothing but a small bag over their shoulder, to visit the local Community Center. (Its childish name, "Morning Star," sticks in my head.) Apparently, they're just going for a long weekend.

For the next few miles, the road runs along a noise barrier so we can't see a thing. "Movement regional HQ," our driver states knowingly into the mic like a city tour guide. She's clearly trying to impress us with her knowledge. As I count the emergency exits in the surface of the soundproof wall, I wonder what I would miss most if I left the Institute. I think it's the power to change destinies, harnessed to a good idea. But for anyone who thinks the work to create a New World is mostly revolutionary combat, terrorist attacks, and shouted speeches, I've got news.

Just then I hear the driver call "Last stop," jarring me back to reality. What I took as an announcement for everyone to get off, though, is actually the name of the Community Center where my last fellow passenger is going. I suddenly feel a pang of regret that I didn't talk to her. Before I can say goodbye, the driver pulls away, and I notice that, from behind, the woman we just dropped off has the same figure as my smoking buddy from the Institute. That starts me wondering if we were in the van together the whole time, and no matter how hard I try to get it out of my head, I can't stop thinking about it.

I sway in my seat as the driver suddenly veers from her lane, cutting off a trailer truck. She acts as if she's transporting things rather than people, and the fact that I ask myself if, ultimately, she really is just hauling junk is a clear sign of my mental exhaustion. Like when the servers at the Institute overheat and the whole server closet smells like pickled vegetables.

I watch the landscape outside my window branching off into streams like tributaries from a river. As the road gets narrower and narrower, I see women dressed in skirts, men in trousers and collared shirts. Clearly, the area is lacking in supervision, and I note down the coordinates so I can make a call from the Community Center once I arrive and notify the staff at the regional headquarters we passed. They need to be alerted that the population here is waltzing around in Old World clothes, probably donning tracksuits only to go to the office or job interviews. I'm sure the proportion of workers employed in agriculture and the trades, sectors known for their tendency to Old World thinking, is higher than average here.

I've always been bothered by the arrogance of city folk, but there's some truth to the idea that progressive thinking thrives best in urban settings, and I see nothing like that around here, even when I press my face against the window to take in as wide a view as possible. Instead, I see a group of women in skirts walking with rakes and a wagon full of hay. As a pair of men stops the women to check their IDs, I want to beat my fists against the glass until it breaks and scream, "You and your old-fashioned clothes, with your trolley carts and male leaders, belong in a museum!"

Maybe the novices from the villages who criticize our documentaries for their bias have a point. Maybe the Institute does have a distorted view of how things work in certain regions.

From time to time, the idea of setting up a "customer support center" comes up for discussion at work. This center would serve the women who call us looking for husbands and partners picked up by an Institute patrol van while they were away, but who, due to bureaucratic snafus, haven't been notified of the intervention. Anyone who didn't reach the operator would hear a recording of soothing music while on hold, and the next level of service would be a line with no operator at all, just music, because what women in this situation need first and foremost is to calm down. I would write down my idea right now if I hadn't already packed my notebook away in my suitcase.

Any minute now, the van should be dropping me off near the Community Center that I'm going to visit (I'm hesitant to ask why the driver doesn't drop us off right at our destinations, but I suspect the reason may be that some locations are classified), and if I had my notebook out I would write, "It's criminal the way we overvalue information and give such short shrift to emotions." Most of the women who call around the Institutes trying to track down their partners are selfish people, incapable of seeing the world from anything other than their own limited perspective. The location of the man in question is secondary to them. What really matters is understanding how they ended up there! An operator-free line with soothing music might help them come to terms with the flood of hurt feelings and see their situation in the context of societal change, so instead of just shouting that one man's name, they might shout about something more meaningful.

I'm so worked up it takes me a moment to realize that the view out the window has changed to swampy marshland. As the van bumps along a narrow track strewn with rocks, there are a few practical details I'd like to ask the driver, but a thin metal partition separates her cabin from the seating area. I can see her shorthaired head jouncing up and down through a small cutout in the metal. I'm sure she's as wrecked from the journey as I am. Why didn't I check the map beforehand to see where this place actually was? The whole way I've been wondering what else I forgot besides the rysol. Now I know what it was.

I unzip the small pocket on my suitcase and fish out a sweet roll I bought at the gas station. The napkin it's wrapped in is soaked in jelly. I wipe my fingers on my pants. They'll issue me a new tracksuit and clean hoodie when I arrive. My T-shirt is soaked through with sweat, and the thought of introducing myself to the section head looking like this appalls me. Maybe I'll even be invited in for a formal five-minute interview with the Community Center director, and as I swig from the bottle of mineral water with Rita on the label, I can almost feel her disapproving frown.

The pioneers of the Movement rode out how many terrorist attacks hiding out in basements, trapped in seemingly hopeless situations, digging their way to freedom with their own bare hands? And here you are, worrying over a jelly-stained uniform. For shame. Movement warriors spent years living like animals, scattered through the forests on enemy territory (though a few of them freely chose to become recluses of their own accord). Even those just a generation older than me penned manifestos in gloves with cutoff fingertips while sleeping in tents on city squares in unsanitary conditions, eating whatever their quiet supporters like my mother brought them, leftovers of family suppers, smuggled out while the head of the family settled down in the living room to watch the dramatic events unfold live on TV, giving the Movement a week, a month, a year of life at best, until their "idiotic demands" were laughed off once and for all—or worse, until women themselves came to realize there was nothing in it for them.

"It's hara-kiri for femininity," the Movement's enemies chortled. They themselves, of course, were incapable of defining what femininity meant, except to protest that "It's not what you all say," while the Movement, for its part, was careful from the very start not to offer any definition of its own.

I myself have no experience from that period of intense struggle in opposition, a fact we also drum into our novices whenever they get haughty: "You came to this as a done deal," the point being to emphasize how much hard work it took to make the society that they now take for granted. Because the natural state of affairs is chaos, injustice, and hierarchy, and when people say "it started with Adam," that includes the gendered disparity in muscle mass, and to return to so-called traditional or conservative values would mean a capitulation to the logic of "might makes right."

I wait till we've been parked a while with

the engine turned off to clamber out of the van. The driver lets loose a stream of profanities as she wrestles with the sliding door. She too is fed up with the long drive, and I think: If she throws a fit like this over such trivial inconveniences, she can't be too well versed in Movement ideology—just like our cooks.

The generation of our grandfathers' grandfathers could fix an engine with a piece of wire bent into a loop, while people today are totally lost if something goes wrong with their car out of reach of civilization, and the representation of real space by the space of social media is complicated by the fact that the virtual world takes up the same amount of time as we supposedly save by using it.

I stand blinking in the sharp sunlight, dragging my suitcase behind me with my left hand as I thank the driver with my right. She points me in the right direction, says "People swim in the lake there," turns, and is gone. I stand amid the open landscape at a loss. All of a sudden the driver's instructions have vanished from my mind, and the sun is beating down on me the same way it did on my first trip to the Institute with this same stupid suitcase, and I curse myself, the same as then, for failing to bring enough water. I'm sure the driver had some in the cabin with her and would have been happy to share.

It's a trying moment until I peer out toward the lake and see what looks to be a group of women splashing in the water, their outlines shimmering in the heat. Something tells me one of them might be Richard's or Libor's wife, so the first thing I do when I reach the lake is ask where their guard is. A woman in uniform rises from a blanket and introduces herself while the other women return to their fun and games, jumping off a stump into the water and tossing around an inflatable ball—village girls, I assume. In response to my inquiry about clients five and forty-two, the guard shoots back the Movement salute and instead of responding asks me to identify myself: accreditation, home institute address, and section number.

Reports have been circulating among Institute staff about alarmingly lax measures at some Community Centers—reports of "inappropriate sharing of intimate details" with clients, having a negative impact on the reeducation process—and while the reports are as yet unconfirmed, much of my nervousness springs from hearing these "racy" stories.

Wasting no time, I begin my report right there on the spot, jotting down, *Welcomed in a highly professional manner* (I promise myself I'll sit down to my memoirs later on), and my intuition tells me it's going to be a quality facility. It may be that the "rumors" about this Community Center originate in the nature of the building itself. Like a shadow cast by an accusation that soils a person's reputation, even if they soon succeed in proving their integrity; like the house of a dead man that no one wants to live in, even though the electricity and plumbing work just fine and the interior is in flawless shape. "Rebirth," the name of the Center I've been sent to report on, is symbolic: it was formerly the villa of an Old World media oligarch, known for throwing wild weekend parties supplied with underage prostitutes. Years ago, one of our more unstable members slit the pompous ass's throat; the Movement took advantage of the incident by using section 345 of the legal code to expropriate the property and convert the building into a Community Center.

As I arrive, women with hoes are grooming a path that leads down an alley with arborvitae on either side. In place of the original Japanese orange trees, which from a local standpoint make no sense, they've planted an apple orchard, and as a novice is summoned to come and take my suitcase (the staff must have seen me coming from the tower of the "small observatory," installed by the former owner as an "intellectual" alternative to a private cinema), I pick an apple up off the ground. An apple like the apple of knowledge (what is unspeakable is best left to roll around the tongue), with the Movement as Eve, offering knowledge for everyone to taste.

The room the novice shows me to has a view overlooking the countryside. In the distance I see snowy mountain peaks, seemingly in a different climate zone altogether, while laid out directly before me is a landscape of technology: a bakery, workshops, a nanofactory, and other buildings whose purpose is impossible to guess at, all rebuilt from the original racing stables.

Client number five, Felicie, is in a state of induced coma, the section head informs me after picking me up from my five-minute interview with the director. The director spoke at length about the perils of success, of "resting on our laurels," an issue that the Movement is dealing with now, due to its unprecedented growth (in recent months, the Movement has firmly established itself in two South American countries known till now for their deep-rooted machismo), and presented me with a new set of wireless helmets (to conduct field testing of new technologies in more intimate settings like this one was standard practice).

Libor's wife lies in a brightly lit room filled with beds, along with other clients, in the building's former attic (converting this space was the final structural modification made to the villa's interior, the section head explains): white on white, head on pillow, arms tethered.

Lending a boost to a client's self-confidence

is NOT treading a fine ethical line, the attending anesthesiologist declares, and the unpleasantness of the situation for everyone involved (reportedly, Felicie, in brief moments of consciousness, has torn out her breathing tube) can be seen in the fact that one fresh-on-the-job novice had a nervous breakdown after only one night and fled back to the capital to finish her doctorate instead; "so these are the aggravated conditions in which we work," the section head concludes.

While Libor vomits daily in the meatpacking plant, his wife Felicie is undergoing a painful process of mental transformation (her sleeping face still reveals the signs of plastic surgery on her nose, chin, and eyelids). The staff wake her once a week for examination, but despite partial improvement (she now regrets the nose surgery), she continues to insist, "I really did want those tits."

"A truly exceptional case of stupidity," the section head says, adjusting the bolster beneath Felicie's head. As though it weren't precisely extreme situations such as hers that we have to thank for all our most important advances.

Meanwhile Richard's wife, Julie, is away with her group in the nearest town for a gynecological checkup. The Community Center is practically just a dollhouse compared to the Institute, but still, they could hire their own gynecologist. I share my thoughts with the section head as she walks me through the building floor by floor (I won't be able to speak to Felicie personally until they wake her from her coma for her regular tests a few days from now), and she explains that the Center's gynecologist walked off the job a few weeks earlier over disputes with management and they haven't been able to find a new one yet. And it wasn't only the gynecologist. The economist and the accountant quit as well.

"We're going crazy with all this paperwork," the section head says. She then apologizes, saying she has a video call with a chronic recidivist currently in solitary, and hands me off to her subordinate.

"The only purely female service we provide, besides tampons, is lactobacillus soap with a neutral pH for intimate hygiene," declares the guard who takes over as my tour guide.

The first phase of reeducation, she says, is to overload the clients with work, like any standard detox. As in chemotherapy, where healthy cells are damaged along with sick ones, any thoughts whatsoever the women might have are destroyed, in a full-scale massacre. The second phase focuses on eliminating niceties. The motto here is "No aesthetic ass-kissing." (That's what the staff call it; officially it goes by the rather more bourgeois-sounding "How to Be Yourself"— the guard says that country women are absolutely wild about it.) This is where clients learn what Rita realized as a child: a New World woman's vision isn't directed back at herself, like a smartphone on a selfie stick, in order for her to evaluate what she looks like to men, but outward into the world, which accepts her just as she is, in every regard (even as a child I felt sorry for the retired women all made up to ride the tram).

"Tracksuits are good for a person's spirituality," the guard declares. She says the number of women addicted to makeup remains surprisingly high (any stashed-away makeup kits the guards confiscate from clients are publicly burned in the yard, a ritual held simultaneously with the veggie wiener roasts in the orchard, a special treat to reward clients for good behavior).

"You'd be surprised how many regions still follow Chinese fashion trends and how many women resist wearing tracksuits. We've got a lot of work ahead of us. That Institute of yours is living in illusion." She looks me up and down with a disapproving eye.

"You systematically overrate women, and the smaller Institutes in the outlying regions are afraid to tell you all the truth. Surely you're aware that half the ideologues who've led the Movement in the past twenty years have been lesbians." She takes a cautious look around, then continues in a lowered voice, "The fact that we aren't allowed to talk about it doesn't change the reality."

"In Rita's case, that rumor was disproven ages ago," I retort indignantly. As if it were even a scandal, as if it made any difference.

A middle-aged woman in a drool-stained hoodie staggers out into the hallway from the clients' sleeping room. "Your group's on snack break. Get your butt to the canteen," snaps the guard (the client is plainly on rysol, if not sordium).

The woman thanks her and makes her way down the stairs, clinging to the banister.

"I'm not saying Rita was a lesbian," the guard says, picking up where she left off. "I'm saying the Movement leadership has always been at least a third lesbians, and when the communities started up and the Movement called for women to leave their families, it was more than half; the members would never have come up with the idea otherwise. Hasn't that ever occurred to you?" She pauses a moment to let it sink in. "Rita was a normal white heterosexual woman, and on top of that she was from a well-off family who passed themselves off as poorer than they actually were."

I feel sick to my stomach.

"There's nothing natural or inevitable about the nuclear family, whether a lesbian says so or somebody else," I fire back angrily. I wonder if I'm dealing with an undercover agent.

"They couldn't say it out loud, but everybody understood."

"What?"

"The instructions to liquidate the male population."

I feel more like I'm talking to a client than a colleague, and for the first time it fully hits me what it means, ideologically speaking, for the Movement to manage such an extensive empire. We must be painting a rosy picture of conditions at the Institute if even just a few hundred miles distant I'm standing with a colleague in an allied facility, in a situation that borders on the ethically unacceptable. I will definitely have to mention this in my report.

I try to counter with a quote from Rita herself, but the guard won't even let me finish my sentence.

"Rita is dead."

"That makes no difference to me or your work," I reply in the only way I can. "Rita lives on through her writing."

"Is this how you imagined the New World? A scam you defend with a slogan?"

We stand face-to-face, hands on our hips, in the villa of a lecherous oligarch who's dead and buried now thanks to the Movement, and instead of congratulating each other, we're practically at blows, for no good reason at all. The employee of an Institute with a budget in the tens of millions and its own brain trust can't be held responsible for the personal beliefs of a guard at some tiny Community Center, so no point in losing sleep over it, I tell myself.

I offer back a friendly smile.

"All these years, the Movement has been hushing up the fact that the problem is mainly with women," I hear my colleague say. "The work of Community Center staff is totally undervalued by the Movement leadership," she adds.

I struggle to hold back a yawn. "How are your finances doing?"

"A lot of ordinary people don't even know we exist. I saw a program about your Institute on TV just last week," my guide says in an aggrieved tone. (They interviewed the director, the section head, and my colleague who smokes. Two clods with a mic and a camera—I passed them in the hall of Pavilion B on my way back from lunch.)

I feel myself wanting to say that our Institute is bigger, and has excellent PR, but instead I just nod my head in sympathy. I'm only here on a visit. Thankfully, I suddenly recall that she started our tour by boasting about the facility's technical amenities. "Can you show me the VR chambers? If you still have time, that is."

We descend the side stairs, then turn left twice, to the wing where the guest rooms used to be, back in lecherous times.

"Here's one. The other one's malfunctioning at the moment. Technology is absolutely fundamental to Rebirth," my guide declares with pride, tenderly petting a pair of virtual goggles. They're connected by a set of wires to something that looks like a towel hook.

I'm embarrassed that the Institute is so far behind when it comes to this sort of thing, though the guard and I both know that innovations, like the new model of wireless helmets, are always tested out first in the smaller operations, so it's really more a privilege than a matter of the Institute being backward (for instance, it spared us the nightmare that resulted when a new line of bugs turned out to be listening in on both sides, to staff as well as clients, completely ruining the careers of the Community Center personnel involved).

The guard straps a pair of goggles on my head and invites me to look around.

"I'm sure you think the people we treat here are the exceptions. That while you at the Institute are busy transforming the species, we're just reforming a few lousy deviants. No. It's all kept hush-hush for political reasons, but what keeps half the Community Centers in business is the outrageous numbers of Old World women who are more or less unreeducatable and kept hidden away in crude, makeshift conditions."

I tried out VR goggles once before, in the game room at my mother's nursing home on my last visit, but the lurch in my stomach bowls me over as if this were my first time. Just like then, I can't see my hands when I look down at them. The one game they had at the nursing home was cricket, and I also tried *Magical Journey*, an interactive tour of an animated park with a cast of fairy-tale characters, the most popular selection among my mother's fellow residents. That uncomfortable feeling of losing your body is something the guard probably doesn't even notice anymore (assuming the staff here use the goggles in their free time like they did at my mother's nursing home, where they used them to play interactive badminton).

"Where are you?" asks the guard.

I don't answer. She should know—she's the one who chose the program.

"There are so many publications out there, whining about how superficial men are. The Movement can't even keep track of them all, let alone prosecute them. But, meanwhile, there's a desperate lack of attention to the fact that what attracts women to men the most is still money and power."

I nod.

"An alarming number of women go damp at the mere offer of a ride in a man's luxury automobile."

She spits.

I examine the detail on individual blades of grass in an impeccably manicured lawn.

"We have to write the manuals ourselves," she says. "The program you're running now is something one of our novices threw together. With no funding, on her own time, after hours. They rejected her grant application because she filled in her genome number wrong."

I'm in a park, the guard's annoying voice reaching me over the chirping of birds.

"We save by cutting back on independent contractors and paperwork. Plus we have to show a loss on our contracts with the actors in our budget forecasts every year, or ..."

I tune her out. I've heard it all before. The quantity of admin required for our contracts with the models we use in our posters and workshop materials is crushing. Outsourcing exhausts us all.

By this point, I'm ready to lie down. Lie down in the nonexistent grass and cover my head with a pillow so I don't have to hear. If the Community Center is having financial problems, the guard should be complaining to regional management, not me. I instinctively swivel my head toward the window in the room (in the goggles, there's a tea rose bush there), thinking as soon as we're done in here I'll go out to the garden and stretch out under an apple tree.

"Is she there yet?" I hear the guard's words

as if coming to me from some faraway land, and I wish I could switch her off, but robot personnel are still a thing of the future as far as our work is concerned (they'll try them out in the backwater centers first too, but by then I'll likely already be retired). In the location where I sense the door, the goggles have an entrance to a luxury estate. Spinning around, I see a swimming pool next to the villa, and stables behind that. Every bit to my liking, in a kitsch historical style—angels and Grecian columns with swans. I make a note to mention it to the guard as an obvious lapse in taste, so she won't think I'm too impressed by the novice's handiwork, when just then a man comes galloping in on a horse, leaps to the ground, and bows, introducing himself as John. He addresses me by name—the guard must have entered my personal data into the system beforehand—and congratulates me on my prestigious job at the Institute. But mostly, he talks about himself, reeling off an inventory of his possessions: forested farmlands and chains of subsidiaries. He's soon replaced by a man in an office with a floor-to-ceiling window overlooking the still-renowned though long-gone Manhattan skyline. He invites me to have a seat ("Get comfortable, gorgeous"), offers me a gin and tonic, then launches into a series of stories about his friends in the film industry (he says he was "totally off his gourd" when he went to Ben Affleck's funeral).

After the third time through the bit with some guy who founded a start-up, I understand the program's logic. The next one is a bank manager who loves scuba diving and Indonesian cuisine, and wants my opinion on buying a house to give me "as a wedding gift." The whole segment ends with a 4D sequence: in one practiced movement, someone pulls down my pants and I feel a tongue shyly exploring between my legs. I can't tell if it's a human or a robot, but I stick with it out of curiosity, letting the program run all the way to the end, including the closing credits and acknowledgements.

"The haptic part was a special bonus, added just for you," says the guard before slipping a turquoise-colored wand into my vagina, presumably to measure my response.

I angrily tear off my goggles.

"We wait until the final exam to spring it on the clients," she adds with a mischievous grin.

As the guard removes the sensor again, smooth and cold, I see a man with his back to me, in a staff uniform, packing his things. So the technology isn't that advanced yet—for that part they still need an actual man. Unfortunately, he leaves before we have a chance to talk (I was hoping to ask what other oral techniques he has up his sleeve).

"You'd be surprised, but even silly things like an Anglo-Saxon name influence vaginal secretions. With Ben and Jake our clients get wet faster and to a greater extent than with Lubomír or Josef. With Roger it's practically instantaneous, as soon as he starts counting off the bedrooms in his villa, and by the time he acquires his TV station more than eighty percent of our clients have damp underwear. Then there's Bill, who's a guaranteed gusher, when he starts in about his jets or the time his father knocked out Zuckerberg's avatar at a party. Same with the next to last one, when he tells how he slept with all the assistants at his law firm."

When I ask which characters trigger the weakest physiological response, the guard mentions Zbyněk, a speech therapist whose hobby is fishing. I'm not surprised. He tells his story while riding the tram home from a course where he's training to be "a teacher's assistant in an interdisciplinary elementary school."

"Not a single drop in any of our clients," says the guard. She adds, in a spiteful tone, "Can you imagine a man not getting erect because a woman is 'just a teacher' with below-average pay? Or popping a hard-on when he sees a woman drive up in the latest model Volvo?"

We sit a moment in silence.

The guard walks off in a huff, then returns with two espressos and a plate of cookies. I attempt to dispel the awkwardness of the moment by stirring my coffee loudly and stuffing my face. After a while, the guard gets up from the table, drags her chair to the wall, climbs onto the chair, and fiddles with something on the ceiling fan.

She sits back down and says in a whisper, "The Movement constantly calls for equality, fighting for the rights of women, who are fundamentally earthly beings." She blows her nose, on the edge of tears.

Only now does it hit me: she was probably deactivating a listening device.

The guard, pulling tissue after tissue out of the box, reminds me of myself the time my mother came to visit and told me, "You've lost a winning battle."

The volume of my sobs that day was louder than the guard's—louder in relation to how much crueler it is to tell someone they've won a losing battle, as my mother obviously meant.

Then again I hear a faraway voice, though the goggles are now off my head and hanging back on the hook: "You passed with flying colors: congratulations!"

The guard waves the sensor in front of my face.

What did she expect? For me to get wet would mean my immediate dismissal. I'm offended she even considered the possibility. How little she appreciates me and how blatantly she makes it clear.

Out loud I say, "Do any of the staff ever climax from those men in the goggles?"

"The diagnostics used to be run manually. Now results are sent automatically from the sensor straight to the client's file in the cloud," the guard replies, noting how much more accurate the new method is. (No information is lost along the way, which happens all the time at the Institute, for example, when a novice gets caught up in conversation on her way to the archive and lays the file down in the kitchen in a moment of distraction, and another colleague picks up the folder by mistake, thinking it's the materials for her workshop, then the novice walks off with the workshop materials, and the section heads go crazy trying to track them both down over the PA.)

Gazing into the chandelier as if hypnotized, the guard declares, "Some women spend years here with no real progress. And then there are the hopeless cases like Felicie. And what was the name of that other one, who's married to your client Richard?"

"Julie."

"Right. She's a scary one too."

Then the two of us just sit there a long,

long time, and neither of us says a peep about anything else at all.

Julie and her group return the next day from their gynecological checkup. The van that drops them off has the same cutout windows as the one that brought me here. I only catch a glimpse of the driver, but she bears a striking resemblance to the woman who drove us here from the Institute.

Maybe they're farther along with robotization than I realized. I promise myself to ask the director of the Institute at our next general assembly. She has firsthand access to Movement leadership.

After checking Julie's papers, I try to get us off to a casual start by talking about how great the VR chamber was. She replies that they were supposed to have the other one fixed by next week, but from the tone of her voice there's no way to know how she feels about the whole thing.

I suggest we take a walk through the apple orchard.

Given that the partners of most of the women here are interned at an Institute, the

Center generally doesn't make a special room available for visits ("We do the best we can with what we have," the section head told me), and, typically, the rest of the family assumes the women just come here to unwind for a while.

"If anyone does visit, they usually just go and stand under the biggest apple tree, out of the rain," Julie says.

I conclude from this that she either doesn't get visitors or, if so, then only rarely, and I feel genuinely sorry for her. I pick up the biggest red apple within reach and hand it to her. She bites into it with a smile.

Then, without any further ado, I get right to the heart of the matter.

"Richard's progress so far is unfortunately disappointing."

I can't stand to beat around the bush. But instead of asking what I mean, she asks what progress he's made, so I'm forced to tell her straight up that her husband's reeducation is "totally stagnant," and though initially I'd said I was here on a "friendly visit," the truth was I had come to Rebirth on business, with the goal of "helping Richard to finally get unstuck." The real reason for my visit, I tell Julie, is to request her cooperation "for the good of his treatment."

"They picked him up without anyone even telling me," she says softly, looking at the ground. "We were getting ready to go to our friends' for the evening. Two hours I waited for him at home, all made up and wearing my dress. I just assumed he'd been held up at work and the battery on his phone had died. Then I called up our friends, sobbing with worry about what might have happened to him, and my friend said she'd heard about men being picked up at work. It had happened to two of her colleagues. And a few days later I heard from someone at the Institute."

"You sat at home waiting for Richard in a dress with makeup on?"

As she lifts her teary eyes, I see something flicker there that threatens to derail our friendly conversation.

"Yes, what else was I supposed to do?"

"Don't you find that embarrassing?"

"It was evening. And our friends live close by. Of course I would have worn a tracksuit if we had gone out for dinner."

"We dress for ourselves, Julie. From what I understand, you used to belong to the Movement just like me."

"Oh, I would hardly say that." She gives a quick laugh and shakes her head.

I could fine her on the spot (the fact that she doesn't regret the offense means the statute of limitations wouldn't apply), but I decide to let it go, a decision that to this day remains a mystery to me.

"What do you mean by that?"

"I don't think I've ever been as unquestioningly enthusiastic about the Movement as you are."

I feel something growing inside me that threatens to cause trouble. My smoking buddy once complimented me on my "impressive" capacity for self-control. Still, it has its limits.

"The tone of your answers speaks for itself."

Eyes pinned to the ground, Julie blurts, "I only wear that hideous tracksuit to go to work, and all the women where I live do the same."

"They do?"

"So did you kidnap them, too?"

"Absolutely not," I answer, stressing every syllable. To refer to the arresting of Old World women and their placement in treatment as kidnapping is not only an act of provocation but—and this is what scares me most—a sign that not even former members of the Movement are immune to the most vicious Old World propaganda.

"I thought it was about freedom. In those days, we all wanted to be in the Movement. It was the hip thing to do when we were back in school, but then ..."

"Then you realized the Movement wasn't just about making demands of men, but you also had to work on yourself?"

"You're nothing but a dogmatist. A fascist dogmatist," Julie mumbles, probably thinking that will make it easier to deny her words later on. So when the going gets tough, which it definitely will, she can object that that wasn't what she said at all, like a typical weak-willed woman. She may just as well have called me an "old fascist dogmatist," bringing the Old World right there into the room with us, in all its ideological glory. In fact it already is. Because Julie just keeps going from there, wading deeper and deeper into the mud.

"I thought it was just about making the world a nice place for everyone," she says. Now, all of a sudden, she speaks slowly and intelligibly, as if carefully arranging items in a display case, but these aren't busts of Rita, like the ones I have in my office at work. Rita would be turning in her grave to hear Julie now. Watching her strike this transparent pose, I can't help but picture Libor, pale and emaciated (I can also hear my mother: "Honey, you're so full of your clients, you don't have room for yourself anymore"), and I say to Julie, "Your 'nice place' is a good start," and then add, surprising even myself with my affable tone, "a good start that leads to a bad end if you think all you need to do is declare the world a nice place without putting any of your own skin in the game. You can't just make demands of other people. You also have to transform yourself."

I can hear the schoolteacher's strain in my voice.

Tossing my apple core on a compost heap

in the corner of the garden, I spy a pheasant hopping around in the bushes on the other side of the barbed wire fence, then another along with it.

"They go there to roost at night, and we envy them that they don't have anyone telling them how to run their lives."

Julie, grimacing, wraps her skinny fingers around the loops of barbed wire that enclose the orchard, but the concentration camp parallel, a Manhood Watch favorite, fails to move me, since, as I explain, "Freedom is inside of you. It's an internal space created out here," and I say it, "by the POLITICS of the Movement, the Movement that you left. Oh, sure, you liked the rhetoric, but you didn't want to sacrifice your comfortable lifestyle, did you? The typical Old World girly-girl way."

I'm just firing off shots at random, but I'm confident it will hit home, because women who boycott tracksuits love to rattle on about equality (the Old World women did too: ranting and raving about injustice while they waited to get their hair done), but it never stops them from seeking out an illegal salon to give them their permanent makeup. A fake face to cover up their insecurities.

"It means giving up a woman's weapons. For fuck's sake, Julie. The disgusting, manipulative strategies of a woman's body that's doomed to get older no matter what she does. Choosing the path of least resistance will come back to haunt you, and the dread will be even worse than before," and as I say this I reflect on the fact that no one has any problem understanding the disastrous consequences of short-term thinking when it comes to elections, but the woefully limited prospects of Old World femininity still have to be stuffed down women's throats even now, and yes, some women end up choking, since nobody's ever taught them to work on themselves before, and I think about how the guard yesterday making fun of the Movement's reeducation of women was damn right.

And Julie just stands there and says, like it's no big deal: "Richard told me ages ago. They want to castrate men, exterminate them, and he was right." I remember Richard telling me the same thing. Relieved that Julie and I at least have that in common, I seize hold of that feeling of relief like the men's balls the Movement has never had any intention of cutting off (and another one of the millions of pieces of evidence that what the Movement wants is structural change, not some silly gender jihad, is the fact that it isn't just Community Center clients who receive gynecological checkups free of charge, but the men in the Institutes also get a comprehensive urological exam for free twice a year), and I turn to Julie, who has finally let go of the wires and stopped playing the Holocaust girl, and ask, "So what did you say back?"

"Naturally, I tried to talk him out of it. I said the Movement wanted equality for everyone. Back then I still believed it, but then, after the regional headquarters kidnapped him and put him in the Institute ... And on TV they lie," she splutters, "they lie that they consult about it with the wives ... But I mean, Richard used to be a total feminist," and for the first time Julie breaks down in tears, her back shaking up and down like a dribbled basketball, which is part of what makes me look up and see one of the section heads watching us out the villa window with a quizzical look in her eyes, and I don't want to cause a stir or do anything that might get in the way of allowing me to talk to Felicie (the director of the Center can withdraw permission at any time), so I wrap my arms around Julie and hold her tight, holding her and rocking her, even when she tries to slip free.

"Julie," I whisper, "Julie, sweetie, we both see things the same when you get right down to it," and I start to hum, but it doesn't help, so I whisper into her ear to just go ahead and cry, "Cry until you let it all out" (meanwhile maneuvering us behind the tree, out of view of the section head), because crying is therapeutic, and a lot of clients see me as tough, but my mother knows the truth, and this will be in my memoirs, that there are times I grieve loss more than anyone—the loss of love, of tenderness, the ordinary passing of life—but in spite of that, or because of it, I will forever remain loyal to my duty. Because everyone chooses and I've made my choice, and the men who call me dogmatic are the ones who want it all, and it isn't until they have to give up their boxer shorts and briefs (at first they think it's just some kind of joke) that they realize ... But by then it's too late.

I maintain a tight grip on Julie, the two of us like a statue reigning over the orchard, a counterweight to the scarecrow at the other end of the garden, keeping the starlings away from the sole cherry tree. One single cherry tree, with its own special bodyguard, and I feel tears in my eyes, too, at the inevitability of it all, because the purpose of my visit is to squeeze Julie like a lemon. Julie who, however fragile her physiognomy, is one of those women who obstinately refuses to understand.

"Richard said the New World wants him castrated," she snivels, wiping her eyes. "Tortured to death." (It's time to end the emotional blackmail of women's tears, the terrorism of those who volunteer for pain, I think as I listen, and despite what my mother says, it isn't that I take things on "out of grandiosity," but that issues like this just keep popping up in front of me all the time.)

The fact that Richard, albeit with varying success, masturbates to a poster of an older woman, in workshop as well as in his sleeping room, is something I keep to myself. At least for now. He hasn't mentioned it in his correspondence with Julie.

In a sense, Richard is actually further along than his wife suspects.

"The thing is to convince him it's not about castration."

"He said he would stop sleeping with me if I didn't leave the Movement."

I kick the tree as hard as I can, but that's not enough for me. I shake Julie like a tree.

"And you fell for that? The birth rate is the highest it's been in decades. You know why? Because women aren't worn out anymore. Because after years of toothless emancipation, they've finally seen a real shift."

Julie stares into the ground, toeing the dirt with the tip of her shoe. She doesn't say a word.

"We've been holding your letters."

Her eyes go wide like she's just jumped out at me from behind the tree, even though the whole time she's been standing right beside it.

"We know everything you write to each other, and you haven't been a support for your husband in his treatment. In fact, your actions have been counterproductive. I came to get a promise from you that you'll change."

The two of us stand face-to-face, each in our own world. My job is to bring them together as soon as possible. In a few minutes we'll be called for dinner. I don't have much time left.

"If you promise me you'll change and tell your husband, too, we'll be able to let both of you go a lot sooner."

"Our apartment ..."

"Don't worry about that. The Movement will give you a new one."

She pauses a moment as if trying to make up her mind.

"What exactly am I supposed to tell him?"

I weigh my next few words carefully, knowing how much is at stake. "Tell him to surrender to reeducation completely and unconditionally. Tell him there's not a single reason not to, and don't you dare mention my intervention. It has to seem like it's all your idea." She isn't capable of the same degree of abstraction as I am anyway. "Apart from that, just write the way you always do. You yourself believe it, so you don't even have to lie. You want to be happy with Richard and he wants to be happy with you. It's up to you if you want to help make it happen."

I go on for another few minutes about how her family's happiness rests in her hands (currently their children are in the care of Richard's parents; due to their young age, their placement in the Gardens was delayed).

As I would later write in my report for the Institute, summarizing all the above in official language, Julie gambled everything in the moment of silence that followed.

"I can arrange for the Movement to issue the highest recommendation on your behalf."

It's the best I can do. I've already exceeded my authority as is. Normally the only ones who can issue recommendations are section heads. But given my good reputation, I figure in this case I can get away with it.

"So what'll it be?" I ask, glancing at my wrist, even though I forgot my watch that morning in the bathroom (the guest rooms were nothing much, and I made a point of saying so in my report). "Yes or no?"

The moment I reach out and stroke Julie's hand (sometimes limbs are more intelligent than even the brain of a New World woman), I know the battle is won.

The women in a medically induced coma at Rebirth have a room of their own in the attic, tastefully designed for that purpose. The Movement takes special pains to ensure that none of its facilities (whether Institutes, Centers, or Gardens) resemble prisons or hospitals. Prize-winning art by elementary school students lines the hallways, floral decorations can be found displayed throughout, and clients' sleeping rooms are adorned with colorful wallpaper (as a reward for good behavior), but in Felicie's room apparently the effort has fallen short.

Despite being bright and sunny (Community Center employees installed the skylight themselves when all the professional craftspeople were called away to work on repairs at a nearby Institute, damaged in an attack by Manhood Watch), it has the unmistakable feel of a hospital room. The odor of disinfectant soap (the bedridden clients are washed by staff every day), the smell of urine draining out of bodies into bags (at Rebirth they recycle it to clean the gardening tools), and the white paper single-use gowns that everyone who enters the room is required to wear for hygienic reasons all combine to overwhelm any attempt to the contrary.

Here in this room, women otherwise viewed as hopeless cases are given the chance to undergo the Movement's educational program. Sooner or later, any sensible person (including me, sitting behind a curtain with a glass of coffee, waiting for them to wake Felicie) has to wonder whether it wouldn't be more effective to use this approach at the Institute, rather than our "schoolteaching" method. Whether it wouldn't make sense to reeducate the rest of the population in a way that is both more transparent and more comfortable for all involved (clients' wake-up times can be predicted and synchronized as needed). In short, whether this room at Rebirth might be the future of the Movement, an experimental harbinger in the DIY setting of a reconverted villa.

To say it didn't occur to me would have

been self-delusion, but to say it was something we might actually introduce at the Institute would have been hypocritical, for one simple reason. The prerequisite for internalizing the defining condition of humanity—namely, the acceptance of interpersonal relations on the basis of equality and a deep nonvisual understanding—is consciousness. The fact that Rebirth staff have nicknamed this room "the crash course" says it all. Intravenously injecting people with software doesn't allow for conscious work on emotions. They are literally just feeding the women a program.

From my position behind the curtain, I survey the faces of the bedridden clients, identical in their lack of expression. The reactions of the Community Center staff confirm my distrust of their treatment method. They say they've observed (the guards agreed at yesterday's dinner) that even though at first glance the clients who undergo this method of reeducation act the same as everybody else in the New World, they show a certain stiffness in situations requiring intimate contact. This reduced ability to improvise is no doubt caused by the difference between an understanding arrived at through work and an array of ideological data pumped into your brain through a tube for you to retrieve later on.

Still, it's better than being "fucked for life," as one of the guards at dinner summed it up. Raising a forkful of tofu to my mouth, I could only agree (in contrast to the damp, untidy guest rooms, the tofu roulade was beyond reproach).

I observe through the curtain as the anesthesiologist approaches Felicie. She sits down on the edge of the bed, removes the IV, and gently pats the client on the cheek. ("We gave her a low enough dosage of tranquilizer this morning that any strong external input should bring her to consciousness," the section head explains as she picks up my empty coffee glass. When it comes to cleanliness in here, no exceptions are made.)

The client sluggishly opens her eyes. "Be prepared for anything," the anesthesiologist says, nodding at me to indicate I should move to the bed. I check Felicie's papers the same as I checked Julie's a few days earlier, though in this case it's mostly pro forma. From her blank stare I can tell Felicie has no idea what's going on. As the anesthesiologist leaves the room, for the first time in ages I get a fierce craving for a smoke. Probably because it's an unfamiliar situation.

At any rate, that's the silent excuse I make to myself for my weakness, while out loud I excuse Felicie for hers. "Your husband says he's sorry for all he's done to you."

Her face jerks toward the wall. I can only assume it's deliberate. Based on the guards' reports, she stands behind her decision to get plastic surgery (except for the nose) and has shown no response to the fact that her husband's bulimia was brought on by feelings of guilt.

"Despite the fact that the client's husband forced her to undergo abdominal liposuction, a quack rejuvenation procedure that caused the client to break out in eczema, and that he himself brought her and signed her in to an illegal plastic surgery clinic, requesting they perform every available beautification treatment, the client denies any wrongdoing on his part and continues to insist that she underwent the operations of her own free will," says the report in Felicie's file, which I've been poring over for most of the past two days.

Over the course of the operations, Libor came to visit once a week in the rear section of a hangar that officially served as storage space for garden furniture, the section head who loaned me the file told me. The surgeon had her in there for just under twelve weeks.

"I guess he didn't realize they couldn't do all the procedures at once," the section head said, laughing her inimitable sarcastic laugh, and the reason it was inimitable wasn't due to the inflection of her voice, but because laughter was the last thing appropriate in light of Felicie's situation. Even more inappropriate than having a cigarette, which for that matter I could step out on the balcony and do whenever I wanted. I'd just have to be careful not to let the door latch shut.

"Your husband desperately needs your forgiveness," I say to the pale, listless face, and I just can't wrap my head around this pair. Libor is the very embodiment of self-reflection, but over the course of the past few months he has literally gutted himself (I have a photo of him in my pocket for Felicie, but I'm hesitant to show him to her in such a wretched state), and it's clear to me that unless I can help him and his wife to reconcile, he'll drop dead within a couple weeks at most, somewhere between his bed and the toilet, as the result of a bad conscience, alias starvation.

Though I don't put any stock in ceremony myself, I remind Felicie of the vows she and Libor took when they got married at their local city hall, "for better or for worse," because better and worse have sunk their teeth into them in a pretty original way, and rarely has originality resulted in a shitshow as big as this. But Felicie just lies there, watching me like a vulture. Like she's ready to peck my eyes out, I think, staring back at her tight-lipped face (the artificial smoothness around her eyes reminds me of an ice rink). The tautness also extends to around her ears, and I've been at Felicie's bedside for at least half an hour now, and she still hasn't said anything other than "It was entirely of my own free will"—as she's stated already a hundred times, according to her file. Not only that but it seems the only reason she regrets having her nose redone is that the hack botched the job (giving her a thin little beak in the shape of a crescent roll).

"Give me the mirror," she barks, just when I think she's finally ready to give in and start talking sense. The only reason they keep a mirror in the drawer is for her, and as I feel my frustration grow I've got half a mind to ask, "And what do I get if I do?" since everyone else at Rebirth did just fine without one, and this whole place is one big crusade against privilege. The moment she sees herself, she bursts into tears.

"You're beautiful," I say, "and for a long time now, Libor has loved you only for your unique personality."

I know from the guard that when Felicie was first admitted, she bit some of the staff and seriously injured them. To me it made sense: while Libor blamed himself, Felicie blamed society.

"All you have to do is sign your name on this letter I wrote for you," I add, handing her a sheet of paper and a pen. She snatches the pen immediately, to my surprise, but then hides her hand back under the blanket, showing no sign of interest in reading what the letter says.

"Self-harm, ranting, jumping out the window," I read in Felicie's file. They didn't know what to do with her except to drug her up. Even I had never come up against such a stubborn case. Why does she insist she decided of her own free will when her husband forced her into the surgeries, I wonder, and what does she hope to gain by it?

The anesthesiologist signals to me that Felicie will soon be falling asleep again. That program they're feeding her must be an absolute mess, I think, and feeling like there's nothing left for me to ruin at this point (Felicie's eyes are slowly glassing over), I pull out Libor's photo to give it one more try.

"This is your husband, and he's begging you for forgiveness." I hold the photo in front of her eyes. Felicie is fading fast.

"I guarantee it's no use," the anesthesiologist told me from the start, but I believed I could make it happen, and at that moment I still did. Either Felicie would admit she had done something dumb and her husband pushed her into it, or she would be moved by how miserable he looked. It may have been naive on my part, but without a pinch of naivete I never could have shoveled all the wagonloads of shit I needed to to do my job.

My last hope is buried by a sharp hacking sound. A foamy glob of spit runs down the photo of Libor's pinched face, and Felicie sinks back into unconsciousness.

The anesthesiologist walks past, flashing a triumphant smile. Everything happened just as she predicted. I feel like I should say something, but the best I can come up with is the absurd request for her to forward my ballpoint pen to me in case it turns up later on.

As a parting gift, the Center staff give me a basket full of apples, and all the guards and section heads come out to say goodbye. The van pulls up right on time, though I haven't even put in a request. I stop in to see Felicie one last time before I go. It's the first time I've ever seen her smile happily. Maybe she's better off this way, after all. At least she can't infect anyone else with her attitude. I'll sign her name on the letter to Libor and we'll see what happens.

"She suffered to make herself beautiful for a man, so they busted the guy, and her along with him. I'd go crazy too," I overheard one of the novices say as she changed Felicie's pillow the day before. Another one lacking in ideological education. And I heard the words of the Rebirth director echo in my head from a few days earlier, warning that the Movement was resting on its laurels, and what better proof of that than employees distorting the concept of human beauty in such a disgraceful way?

I shake hands with everyone who came to wish me goodbye. Gripping Julie's hand in mine for longer than anyone else's, I convey it all in my eyes: the promise of a recommendation, a place to live, and a job. There were thousands of empty apartments left behind by men who had cashed in their chips while they were at the Institute and whose wives had gone off to live in communities, which not only made housing accessible to couples who successfully complete their reeducation (I expect Richard and Julie to have no problems passing the final exam), but for Julie also meant plenty of opportunities to find a job in real estate, where she had worked before.

It's all up to you two now, I tell her with my eyes, and I don't look away until the van honks its horn.

3

I wedge the basket of apples in between the spare tires in the luggage compartment so they won't spill along the way, and announce my destination to the driver, just to be safe: "Oskar Nursing Home."

The wheels kick up so much dust that all I can see out the windows is the outline of the bush, and the way the branches smack against the sides of the van you would think no one had ever taken this road before, like a route through some impoverished region in the outer reaches of Eastern Europe leading to the opulent villa of an oligarch. Just the opposite of my trip to the Center, the road network now is like streams flowing into a river, as single-lane roads merge into two-lanes, then highways, and finally, in mid-afternoon, a divided highway with heavy traffic in both directions.

I feel guilty that I've been neglecting my work on my memoirs, even though I swore to myself on the way to the Center that I would make time for them while I was there. But between my grueling interviews with the guards and the previews of the Community Centers' annual theater festival, not to mention the veggie wiener roast, I hardly even had time to write up my report for the Institute. My detailed description of Phase Seven, the final exam, is still nothing more than an intention, and even when I do pull my laptop out, trying to focus on the screen what with all the bouncing around makes me sick to my stomach (like when I used to read in the back seat of our car as a little girl with my mother speeding down the road to wherever it was we were going that day).

My mother now, unlike me, has all kinds of time to read books, and I think there's something about the ancientness of paper that connects it to humanity, just like the Movement's emphasis on authentic interpersonal relationships, and the fact that rare books are a collector's item is proof of their inherent worth, because great things always come from the margins, just like the Movement, and they become great through the hard work of a small community of enlightened individuals, who usually come off as ridiculous at first, which is one of the obstacles that has to be overcome.

The fear of looking ridiculous, by the way, is often the greatest fear that people have in prosperous countries, where the mortal fear of whole cities being ransacked by war has given way to the normalized fear of terrorist attacks by groups fighting for a cause (contrary to popular belief, Rita's sources of inspiration for the Movement did not include the Red Army Faction, though there were some vague similarities in wording). The Movement soon overcame this fear, so, for most people, Manhood Watch were the ones who looked ridiculous. Insisting on their breathless defense of the Old World, they got caught up in the very ridiculousness that they tried to attribute to the Movement. The ridiculousness not of failing to understand the great ideas of someone considered ridiculous by narrow-minded fools, but of considering something great only because it makes no sense (instead of evaluating a woman based on the words coming out of her mouth, they did it based on the color of her lipstick)—and the ridiculousness the Movement struggles with in its own ranks is the women who never cease to embarrass us. I think about all this as I gaze out the window at the slew of innovative construction projects (featuring hanging gardens of vegetable plants and flowering orchards, the crops sold out of ground-floor shops, and, thanks to regional self-sufficiency, the ecological footprint caused by the transport of crops from one end of the earth to the other is not only shrinking but actually neutral, since the upper-floor inhabitants of these colossal structures carry the harvest down to the shops from the hanging gardens in baskets themselves, with the money grossed from the sale of the crops handed over to the management company in place of rent). Observing the purposeful hustle and bustle (in some places, they pass the baskets down a human chain, the next-to-last person in line rinsing off the fruit and the last one carefully depositing it in trays that then go straight to the sales outlet, no more than fifteen feet away), my heart rejoices to see such solidarity. Meanwhile I listen in on the conversations among my fellow travelers, returning to their Institutes after visits just like mine.

A colleague behind me is telling her seatmate about a recidivist she was working with who declared that her youth and physical beauty were her pride and joy, rather than something to be ashamed of (as if the Movement ever believed a person's appearance was shameful, rather than simply one aspect among others whose importance was shamefully overrated). "If you're so smart," she had told the guard, "then why don't you endow me with something else that works on men? You heartless bitch."

The woman telling the story is holding a basket with a goose on her lap (there's something sweetly idyllic about the way the Centers load us up with their products on our visits), and between the goose's honking and the music on the radio, which the driver put on without asking any of us (the type of rudeness that really pushes my buttons), I can't quite catch everything my colleague is saying: "... even packed her study guides, but I doubt she'll take any of them with her. She's already failed so many times. Sure is a hit with the guys, though." Right, the boneheads who keep worming their way out of reeducation, I think, the dimwits who intentionally don't understand (more than eighty percent of men nowadays have been smart enough to open their eyes), a species drawing closer to extinction with each passing year (every day our patrols reduce the number bit by bit). Coordinated reeducation for both sexes is the foundation of the Movement, and the fact that this is what I've been dealing with for the past few days at Rebirth tempers my hostility toward the recidivist (either way, women like you are history, so enjoy profiting off your visuals while you can). I feel a flood of compassion, remembering Rita's words of solace to members of the Movement who struggle with similar women, because our greatest challenge isn't recidivist men, but the women who undermine our work with their open contempt for our values.

You don't speak for us, feminist fascists—I

remember the poster from the protest of Old World women that I marched in as a little girl (like an anarchist visiting a Nazi grave), an image I had blocked from my memory for years, because as soon as I saw the posters I ran away, fleeing in tears from that demonstration of Old World shallowness, with its rejection of lofty ideals in favor of its own ugly selfish interests. Even now, sitting in the van between two bags of vegetables (one of eggplant, the other overflowing with shiny tomatoes), I can still picture it like it was yesterday. I walked all the way home that day, rather than taking the tram, because my tears just wouldn't stop. In fact, the longer it sank in the worse it got. And this is what Rita had to say about the "sisterly rift," which some troglodytes still use to this day to try to disparage the Movement: "Let us have compassion rather than hatred for the women who cannot capitalize on their inner qualities, and who, instead of caring for their own inner being, devote themselves to their exterior. They are like a cabinet ceaselessly wiping the dust from itself, rather than taking the time to study the books housed within.

They do so out of intellectual laziness, out of a superficiality which nobody can blame them for, since they were raised that way. Others were born foolish, and foolish they shall remain. And then there are those women who truly have nothing to offer the world except their surface, so they care for that surface above and before all else, as a mother dotes on her only child."

Something catches in my throat, something I can neither swallow nor express, and sitting there in the van I am overcome with tears in a way I haven't experienced since that long-forgotten protest. I hold my head in my hands, tears running through my fingers, dripping down onto my thighs. Dark splotches form on the gray cotton of my tracksuit, like the ones you see on clients being dragged down the Institute halls, peeing their pants in fear of the electroshock helmet. As the tears soak through the fabric, a damp stain spreads across my lap, and as they filter into the curls of my pudendum I can feel the moisture on the lips of my vagina, since even though nobody asks or expects it of me, I don't wear underwear either, out of solidarity with my clients. And the tears keep flowing, until everything around me is swimming. The scenery outside the window, the vegetables, my colleagues, even the shabby seat covers. It all blends together, shapeshifting into creatures, half human, half beast. I see desert oases and arching shapes that I don't want to call breasts, helmets, and buttocks, but they are, and a mouthful of animal teeth sneers at my weeping as something so cheap and absurd it could never be anything but ridiculous. Like the consequence of some age-old misconception, and I want to push my way through the bushy clumps of those stains to reach it, to find that mistaken thought at the place and time it occurred, but nothing else in the world has ever scared me so much. The sneering isn't from outside, the whole thing is internal. And like a rock wall splitting apart to reveal treasures hidden deep within, I see something opening up inside of me: a gap in the seams of my continental plates, cities being swallowed whole, their shrieks and roars drowning in the flood of debris, the notch of my sex hewn with a dull ax. And I hear my colleague's voice: "Hey, look, a new sodium palace," but it sounds like it's coming to me from far, far away, and soon after that, I fall asleep.

I still don't feel totally normal when my colleague sitting across the aisle asks with a serious face who I think was trying to poison me "with that veggie sausage you ate," but I laugh along with everyone else. I know veggie sausages aren't poisonous, since they eat them at Rebirth whenever they have a cookout in the community garden, roasting them over a fire of confiscated makeup, but just to be on the safe side, I give a call to the director of the Center to ask about the sausage they gave me for the road, but she doesn't pick up.

We drive all night and into the next day, and some of my colleagues get off and new ones get on, and some of the rest stops and intersections have employee vans waiting at them (my colleague with the goose boards a van parked on the roadside in the middle of nowhere), and the system is as well organized as the postal service in ancient Rome, only instead of horses delivering us, we're transported by closemouthed drivers, and at the rest areas where we stop to throw out our rotten vegetables and have a snack, we run into people, and they're people from the New World, and it's a beautiful thing.

And just like last time, after a while we exit from the main road, and this part I enjoy, because last time my view was blocked by the noise barrier, which keeps people on the other side from having any direct contact with modern civilization (one colleague claims it's an autonomous free-trade zone, another says it's the future site of a space shuttle center, but the giant *KLONNING* spray-painted on the wall by a street artist suggests it's a center for assisted reproduction). Then, like a jump cut, the wall abruptly comes to an end and we're in the midst of untamed countryside, the wild vegetation growing thicker and thicker as the road narrows, turning bumpy (the leaves on the burdock plants are big as umbrellas, and judging from the tangles of old trees, there's zero interest on the part of local developers), and once again I'm the van's only passenger, and I remind myself not to repeat the same rookie mistake as last time, and when the driver lets me out and helps me with my suitcase, I ask if she has a bottle of water she might be able to spare.

My mother's nursing home, for family members of Institute staff, is also a property with a rich history. A donor from a nearby town, a successful businesswoman in communications, funded the conversion of local buildings into Institutes, Centers, and Gardens. For retirees she negotiated the purchase of a long-abandoned motel (credit for the idea of building a motel in seclusion belonged to a man with the initials DB, but shortly before it was finished he was admitted to the Institute, and allegedly he didn't live to see the opening of the retirement home two years later).

Whenever I came to visit, my mother and I always enjoyed speculating about what might have happened to him. A year ago, she even asked if I could try to dig up more information ("You've got connections," she said, trying to butter me up), but the Institute's historical records were silent on the matter. When people disappear like that, it makes it look like the Movement doesn't consider their lives important, but DB would never have left such a lasting mark on the history of the region with his dubious motel as he did, through no effort of his own, with the respectable senior center (stranded out in the middle of nowhere, the motel would have gone bankrupt within a year, my mother and I agreed).

At my request for water on exiting the van, the driver pops back up to her seat and grabs a six-pack of two-liter bottles, which I politely decline. "A half-liter of Vacek's mainstream mineral water will do," I say. I'm sure the vans stock that brand. I've seen it on TV. Slipping the bottle into my kangaroo pocket (the dilemma over whether to make the Movement hoodies with one pocket in front or two on the sides nearly paralyzed the clothing division for several months), I grip the handle of my suitcase in my right hand, carrying the basket and two plastic bags in my left.

Julie must be having a laugh, picturing me loaded up like a Christmas tree. At the last minute before I left Rebirth, she crammed a few extra items into my bags. And now, as I watch the van roll away in a cloud of dust, I think: I don't care if she never remembers me again, just as long as she writes Richard.

"Věra, darling!"

My mother stands erect as a tree, gripping the shaft of a two-wheeled cart. "Come here and let me have a look at you."

"Mom," I say, my voice dropping, "what are you doing here?"

But she's already loading the plastic bags into the cart and helping me with the suitcase, practically shoving me out of the way.

"Did you travel alone?"

"Only the last few hours."

"I feel sorry for whoever rode with you, then. I can smell the sweat on you from a mile away. Blow your nose," she says, handing me a handkerchief.

It totally slipped my mind to pick up my new tracksuit at the Center, but there really wasn't time.

My mother never knows exactly when I'm going to come, but she somehow senses it every time. I always run into her on the road. Last time she was sitting under a tree, even though it was well after midnight. Her usual explanation is that she "went out for a stroll."

"I've been up to my ears, you know," I say in defense of my dirty tracksuit.

"You've been up to your ears ever since you went to work for them."

I stop for a second, trying to think how many years it's been, but I can't come up with anything that stands out as a landmark.

My mother starts off, pulling the cart, and I spend a moment fighting over the handle with her in vain.

"So, what's new?" I ask.

I can see the alley of trees along the road have grown a bit since last time, but my mother still looks the same. Compared to her I often feel like I'm the one getting old, and she's just sitting waiting for me to come and move in with her, so we can live together like we did all those years before I started work at the Institute.

"We have a herd of goats out back," my mother says. "The director's lost her mind. She says we need something to take care of. Active relaxation, she says. As if old age was supposed to be hard labor. You think they've got this at other homes?"

I tug the cart bumping along behind me. I wonder where my mother got hold of it. I doubt it belongs to the nursing home, but the next closest place is a gas station two miles away. Then there's a village a bit down the road, but I know she doesn't go there.

"Would you like to move somewhere else?" I ask. Complaining about the home is my mother's favorite pastime.

"If you happen to know of anything …"

I'm willing to go through it all again—the paperwork, the requests, the forms. I want her to feel better. The problem is, there's always something. My mother will always complain.

"How's Jaroslav?" I ask instead.

My mother waves dismissively. "He doesn't want to go anywhere. The casino and mushrooming, at most. And even then, he'll only go to the glade by the swings. Those are his 'spots,' as he likes to say. The forest's a slog, what's the point? You're gonna get fat, I tell him."

"He already is, isn't he?"

My mother stops and looks out over the countryside.

"Want to take a rest?"

She shakes her head and asks for a cigarette, then lights up and stands staring off into the distance.

"They're gonna build over there," she says.

"By the pond?"

We stand a moment in silence. She stamps out her cigarette and slips the butt in her tracksuit pocket. I've long since given up commenting on her manners.

We greet the elderly men and women sitting in chairs around the tables out in front of the home. My mother is so proud of me, she introduces me to her same friends every time. I recognize one of them sitting next to the perfectly weeded flower bed.

"So, have you rounded up all those bastards yet?" my mother's friend asks. "They been giving you trouble? I'll show them if they start acting up with a nice girl like you."

She jokes around with me the same way every time.

"We haven't got them all yet, but it won't be long. There's almost no place left for us to put them anymore."

"Yep, it's like I always said. The Movement

will take care of it. Am I right or am I right?" The old woman laughs as my mother and I park the cart.

Without bothering to ask, my mother takes a large cucumber out of my supplies and waves it in her friend's direction.

The old woman reciprocates the suggestive gesture. "You wouldn't happen to have a nice big fat banana in there, would you?"

She and my mother laugh uproariously. I'm glad to see my mother in such good shape. She and the other woman are probably the same age, but you'd never know it to look at them.

"You've got a good crew here, Mom," I say as we finally sit down. My mother takes off her sunglasses and pulls out another cigarette, this time from her own pack, which she went and got from her room. I still have mine in my pocket, but I wait to see if she'll offer me one of hers.

"Did you get that promotion?"

"The General Assembly hasn't approved it yet." It irritates me that my mother is bringing this up.

"You said it was up to the section head and

that you were on good terms with her."

"Yeah, but they still have to vote on it."

"So it's a formality." She smiles, patting me on the shoulder.

As the sun sets, I try in vain to remember the last time I just sat somewhere like this. I watch the clouds turn orange as streaks of red spread across the sky. Even though we're in a secluded location, due to the light pollution from the nearest town the stars are only faintly visible, if at all. Plus, every time I come my mother complains that she has trouble falling asleep because of the traffic on the highway, which I know is nonsense, but when I wake up in the middle of the night, I strain so hard to listen that I practically foam at the ears, so maybe she's right after all.

"It combines the worst of the city with the worst of the country," my mother once said, describing the benefits of the location. That was the first and last time I ever came to see her with a man. I broke up with him less than two years later, when neither of us was willing to relocate. I told him there was a double studio free at the Institute, since he was always saying how he could work from anywhere. Apparently not.

"So, how's that new guy of yours?" my mother asks as if reading my mind. Nobody else can do it like she does.

She stubs out her cigarette with a sigh, stretching her legs onto the empty chair beside me.

"Has he come to visit yet? Or are you still just talking on the phone?"

From the way she massages her calves, I can tell she wants me to ask about them. In her emails she complains of cramps that wake her in the night, but when I suggest seeing a doctor she just waves dismissively.

"I went. About a month ago."

As the air cools, I wrap myself in a blanket stamped with the Movement's red logo. Each chair here comes with its own personal blanket, folded neatly over the backrest. It's details like these that reassure me: whatever my mother says, the home provides excellent care.

"Out in that backwater town of his where they don't even have their own grocery store?"

"He came and picked me up from the train," I add, as if I had any obligation to explain. She'll never stop, and I'll never let her know how much it gets to me.

My mother's friend gets up from her chair and walks back into the building, wrapped in a blanket. As she passes, she pulls the cucumber I brought with me out of her pocket and waves it in my face.

"Feel free to stop by if you want to borrow my boyfriend for the evening," she says, and she and my mother burst out laughing again.

I make a bet with myself whether my mother will start back in with it later tonight or wait until tomorrow. I've had it up to here with her shallow vulgarity.

"He came to pick you up from the train, and then what?" she asks, and I can practically hear her say: *There's only one thing to do out there in the sticks anyway*, but she would get hugely insulted if I suggested that's what she was thinking, and she would never admit to it anyway.

The next morning, right after breakfast, my mother suggests we go see the goats. "They like this grass the best," she says, tearing a handful from next to the fence. It's the same grass that grows everywhere. My adamant silence in certain situations is both a cause and a consequence of our disharmony. My mother derides my quiet defiance as "immature," and there's probably some truth to that. She's always been a celebrity, and growing up with a celebrity inclines one in a certain direction: it both shrinks and refines you at the same time, and does so through a mechanism which, unlike sex, it's absolutely impossible to talk about with my mother ("My biggest mistake for the longest time was disqualifying men with crooked dicks," she said last time I saw her), because, for all her vaunted openness, the way my mother "is" prevents her from looking at what she's not and never will be, no matter how hard she tries.

At most she suffers pangs of conscience, which are totally beside the point, I think, watching her stretch her wrinkled hand through the slats of the fence and seeing the look of childish delight that spreads across her face as the goats tear the grass from her hands. Meanwhile she hums the tune to a song I've never heard. A song from a world all her own. "If it hadn't been that, it would've been something else" is an attitude I've inherited from her, and in my mother's case it's connected to feelings of guilt that she didn't support the Movement more actively in its early days. She never stepped out of the "gray zone of quiet supporters," even though, or maybe because, she always backed my involvement one hundred percent, and, unlike my colleagues' mothers, who my colleagues spend long hours in the kitchen analyzing—feeling they were pressured into decisions that they weren't convinced were the right ones—my mother has always given me complete freedom in everything I've done.

"Are you happy?" she asks out of nowhere.

My arms are full of grass.

"I am."

This answer of mine, delivered the same way each time in response to my mother's regular question, has acquired all sorts of connotations and meanings over the years, and mostly what it reflects is the gratification I get from my work on a sheer biological level (people are constituted by ideals, so everyday work on their behalf satisfies a primal need), though every now and then I've also been gratified by my relationships with men (there have even been brief periods when those relationships were more important than anything else), and feeding the last goat, a scruffy little black thing, my mother says, "Just the day before yesterday I was remembering that one who begged you to quit your job and go away with him," and I wonder why instead she doesn't remember the one who briefly worked as an instructor (especially since he shared my mother's interest in Baroque painting), or the one who lived with me a whole three years in my studio and irritated my mother with his passion for airplanes. Then out of the blue (there was probably thunder and lightning, but we were too busy feeding the animals to notice) it starts to rain, the biggest downpour we've had in months.

I grasp my mother's hand and the two of us go racing back to the nursing home (from the goat pen it's only a short distance, but to reach the entrance you have to circle almost all the way around the fence). My mother swears ("I was hoping to go to the pond next, but now it'll be fucking mud," which makes me glad, since I never did understand what my mother saw in that vine-choked pond—you can't even swim in it), and that makes us both laugh, and no sooner do we reach the doorway of the home (my mother's wet hand keeps slipping out of my palm) than there's a terrifying thunderclap like the kind you hear in the movies. Like a harbinger of something awful about to happen, but the difference between reality and the movies is that in real life thunder and lightning don't mean anything other than, as my mother remarks, "Good thing we had them put in that second lightning rod this spring," and I blame it on the guilt I feel about putting off work that I jump straight from reality and the movies to my own personal resolutions, and my hands tingle as I think about the fact that I haven't touched my memoirs since the day I left the Institute. Shame on me.

By the time we reach the lobby, the way the water is streaming off of us you would have thought we had fallen in the pond (which I hope doesn't happen to my mother on one of her nighttime "strolls"), and the moment we enter the common room, which you pass through to get to the bedrooms on the second floor (even with the renovation, it's obvious from the layout that the building used to be a motel), Jaroslav, who's been sitting in there watching TV, jumps up to welcome us. He starts right in drying my mother's head with a towel he has all ready to go, and promptly sends me off to her room to bring her down a dry tracksuit.

On my way back from my mother's room, I see Jaroslav through the bead curtain in the room with my mother, saying, "You know you aren't supposed to bend over, dear." He's crouched in front of her, as if he were proposing, tenderly untying her shoelaces. (She can't even take off her own shoes anymore?)

My mother has the towel wrapped across her chest, and as the two of them see me standing in the doorway, they both explode in laughter.

"You look like a sausage," my mother chortles as Jaroslav helps her change clothes, and I feel a cruel urge to tear off the tracksuit

I borrowed from my mother's wardrobe without her permission and tell Jaroslav about her crude cucumber-banana jokes (would he have laughed too?). Just then another retiree enters the room and asks my mother, "So, is she here yet?" as if I wasn't standing right there next to her, and I wonder whether my mother has something going with this man too. The way she smiles at him, I wouldn't rule it out. It's the same way she smirked at me in my early puberty, when I still lived with her, and I came home one day to find her in the kitchen, naked, with a naked man, and she casually said, "Daughter, this is your father. He lives in Tábor, so unfortunately he can't raise you," and she always spoke of him with respect as the love of her life. I wonder if Jaroslav knows about him, and suddenly, for the first time in my life, it occurs to me that when she said he lived in "Tábor," she may have meant "tábor" with a small *t*, in other words a camp, which is what Institutes used to be called when my mother was young, and I decide I'll have to ask at some point, because lies that might be true, and vice versa, are my mother's main stock-in-trade.

"Yes, everything's going according to plan," I tell the man after my mother introduces us and he asks about the Institute's work with the "forest refugees." I forget his name as soon as he tells me, but not the fact that he has a daughter in the nearby Community Center and a son in the Institute a hundred and twenty miles away. He says his daughter ("the family disgrace") has been in treatment at the Center for over two years, and his son is the manager of the Institute canteen.

"I'm here thanks to him," the man says proudly, adding that last year his son even received the Rita Medal for Best Employee. He then starts rattling off the benefits of living in the old folks' home: field trips "to absorb culture," comprehensive, discreet care, and he's especially excited about the plans to install a pool and offer residents special swimming lessons for "reconditioning" (the nursing home's director is a former member of the national water polo squad, an "often neglected" sport, as the man emphasizes).

"Your mother would have made a beautiful

synchronized swimmer, and now she'll have the chance. They're going to have that pool built within two years. The director gave me her word," he says.

"We can't even imagine what it would be like here without your mother," the man adds. Apparently he's forgotten my name as quickly as I've forgotten his.

My mother blushes like a little girl, and Jaroslav frowns.

When the man retires to his room ("I take my medicine at twelve," he says apologetically), my mother asks Jaroslav to bring her a mug of tea to warm up, saying, "It was cold as a kennel out there in that awful downpour, honey." I grab Jaroslav by the elbow on his way out and ask him to bring a mug for me, too.

The main advantage of my work is that I can travel light. My mother eats some of the apples and vegetables I brought from the Community Center and gives the rest away to her friends. What little is left goes to Jaroslav. "He can add it to his pickled mushrooms," my mother says, and Jaroslav, overhearing, gives me a whole jar of mushrooms to take back with me to the Institute. He insists on wrapping it in three issues of the Movement's old magazine and wedging it into my suitcase himself to make sure that it won't break.

The patrol van is waiting for me in the same spot where it dropped me off, and if I weren't squeezed so tightly into my mother's tracksuit ("You can bring it back next time, or I'll pick it up when I stop by") that it was practically strangling me, I would burst into song. As much as I'd been looking forward to taking a few days off when I left, I'm even more eager now to get back to work. Running through my clients in my mind, I can't wait to see the progress they've made (sometimes even just a few days can work wonders). It even warms my heart to think about my smoking buddy, tormenting me with her loud music and constant requests to borrow my lighter.

Every time I visit, my mother makes at least one comment I can't forgive her for, and this time it's: "I don't understand how someone with such a social mother has no real friends at work and has never been able to stay in a relationship with anyone." She makes the comment just before we say goodbye (she was going to lug my suitcase to the van all by herself again, but Jaroslav knew her tricks and beat her to it), and we're a few bends down the road before I can get it out of my mind (no, I'm not social, and I'm not easy to live with, but I'm old enough that I fully accept myself as I am), and besides you can't be much help to your clients if you're caught up in yourself, as I figured out ages ago. And for the rest of the day, the Czech countryside brings me almost nothing but joy.

Looking out the window, I have the feeling the New World is even more well entrenched than it was when I left. I don't see a single person not wearing a tracksuit. The one exception is a woman who looks like a textbook Old World prostitute standing by the side of the road, and for hours after I wonder if she was just acting in a historical movie shoot, or if she really was a walking museum piece, a creature from the benighted realms. Had I witnessed one of the last survivors of a dying breed, or just a new wave of satirical retro cinema? (Apparently, some younger members of the Movement dressed up as prostitutes at the solstice and engaged in all sorts of discursive horseplay.) But whatever the case, let it be judged by someone gifted with a truly holistic perspective, which is something I aspire to in those moments when my mind is on fire, although of course I'm too shy to admit it.

The other thing on fire is the inside of the van, which, as I already mentioned, doesn't have air conditioning, and the more stifled I feel in my mother's tracksuit, which cuts into my hips and breasts (in the Old World I would have been gawked at because of how big they were), the more sausage-like I feel and the more it reminds me of the director at Rebirth. I still haven't been able to get hold of her about my possible food poisoning from the makeup-seared veggie wiener. The closer we get to the Institute, the stronger I flash back to that state of gloomy delirium I suffered, and I dial the Center again, but she still doesn't pick up.

I sense that the "food poisoning" was just a cover for something deeper down, related to my crying after the women's protest where they denounced the Movement as fascist. And suddenly it's as clear as the oversize license plate on our van that something inside me is accusing me, and the accusation it's making is that it's being accused, and I could blame it all on something else, but that's the last thing I want to do ("Integrity will get you furthest in life," as my mother taught me growing up), and by the time we're thirty miles away from the Institute and I vaguely recognize the outlines of the landscape, I feel a tightening in between my legs, and judging from the pain it's probably a combination of bladder stress from dehydration and the overly tight track pants.

In the space of just a few seconds, it all comes back again. The notch hewn with a dull ax, the landslides and the shifting earth tumbling into the channel of my wound in the form of ash (the man I was with the longest, who I genuinely loved, said "When I die, I want you to pour me straight from the urn into your vagina"), and squeezing my thighs tightly together I know: the one thing I detest almost as much as hypocrisy is women who make a scene when they get their periods. Because menstrual blood, which at one point was treated like a charm with magical powers, is basically colorless and odorless. It's not about the blood, but the wound from which it issues, the wound behind the blood. And like the cloud of ink a cephalopod releases to confuse its enemies, like a child hiding behind her hands so the world will stop pointing its finger at her, at least for a while, from the murky depths to the dizzying heights and back, I rummage through the heaps of mined slag, the underground seams pillaged of their contents.

When we stop for gas at the rest area, the driver says she has the feeling we've met somewhere before, while the whole time I've been enjoying having somebody new, and I wonder if maybe it's just a bug in the program. A software gimmick that didn't land where it was supposed to, but instead came back like a boomerang, so I just nod and agree: "Probably on one of my last business trips," and the sharp pain in my belly makes my smile a little forced.

The driver kindly hands me a cup of hot

water, and I hear the barking echo of my mother's voice saying how asocial I am and uninterested in the things that others pay attention to (I do keep more than an average distance from most people), and I admit: my relationship to society is closer than my relationships to the individual beings in it, but by the same token, if my mother ever got so lonely in the old folks' home that she actually insisted on requesting a transfer, I would make sure she was moved somewhere else, no matter how many times I had to grovel before the section head, flaunting my spotless record and (indisputable) professional accomplishments while exaggerating my mother's (modest) contributions to the New World.

As the tea diffuses through the water (just to be safe, I take my urological tea with me everywhere), I watch the steam rise from the surface of the cup. Ultimately, whatever pangs of guilt I have are always cleared away by hard work, just like the rain gave way to sunshine after that crazy downpour with my mother, and we embark on each new stage of life more mature as a result of the experiences we've been through. I wouldn't be writing my memoirs otherwise. If I hadn't stood the test. That's more or less how I'd sum it all up. The motto of my life story.

4

Phase Seven, our final exam, starts with the idea that everything that came before is forgotten. The posters the men use for their training are removed from their rooms two or three weeks before they undergo the exam. In the case of clients who've spent years in reeducation, this leaves behind a bright spot on the wall, like the kind you see after taking down a painting (like the one Richard and Julie will hang when they move into their new apartment, previously occupied by a client fallen in the battle to remake himself). Some clients cover up the spot with their wardrobe, ashamed at having taken so long to complete their transformation, while others take pride in it, drawing a frame around the spot in thick black marker, to show off to everyone else, and then again there are men so overjoyed at the prospect of release that they make the mistake of believing it's a done deal. They don't know about the penis stimulation test. The Institute hasn't always used it. But prior to its introduction, no more than one in five of our clients passed the final exam, which was not only a waste of our and others' resources, but also took a toll on the clients themselves. There's no point in a man undergoing the exam unless he has the necessary prerequisites to succeed, and the penis stimulation test rules out those who are unprepared. We don't let anyone take the exam unless they are able to pass, and while this rejection can be devastating for some (our client Jiří, who hanged himself, was just one of eight this last season), it's nothing compared to the frustration that comes from failing the exam. For one thing, nobody but the clients themselves finds out if they flunk the stimulation test (in general, very few people are likely to share that they failed at something if nobody knows the results except them), apart from maybe their roommates—the usual excuse for clients who pull out of the final exam is to say it was for health reasons or that they just weren't feeling ready. Whereas when a client fails the final exam, everybody there knows. Not only do people flock to attend the event from all over the area (the Institute's PR department takes quite an original approach to publicizing our exams), but the clients' wives and their relatives descend en masse from all corners of the empire, and we wholeheartedly congratulate each and every family fortunate enough to celebrate success (for instance, smoothing the way for spouses to advance in their careers, although it isn't official policy and the Movement opposes clientelism), while doing all we can in advance to prevent the clients' failure.

The evening before a penis stimulation test is planned, the client's assigned guard (with permission from the section head) instructs the nurses to add two to three teaspoons of rysol to the client's supper, depending on their body mass. Clients are selected for testing strictly on the basis of their preparedness, as demonstrated in workshops as well as on the guards' evening rounds, when the men masturbate to the posters on command. Each client's progress is scrupulously documented in his file, so that the poster on his wall is taken down only when the model's age no longer has any influence on the client's ability to obtain an erection, having been surpassed by his intellectual appreciation of the model's inner qualities. Unfortunately, even those who end up faring badly on the test are capable of holding forth on the inner beauty of women when woken for an evaluation in the middle of the night. The point is that, unlike the practice routines with the poster, it isn't just a matter of understanding and internalizing the New World worldview that a woman's attractiveness is unrelated to her age, but of demonstrating immunity to anything that makes a woman, or any of her body parts, a means for the soulless satisfaction of primitive desire.

Assuming the transformation from Old World to New can be called a leap in discourse, and we've seen for ourselves now a thousand times over that that's precisely what it is, then the Institute's final exam is a leap in discourse par excellence. A leap within a leap, like a gymnastics routine: you either totally nail it or walk off the floor sobbing into a towel. But while gymnasts have a coach who can give them feedback on what they did wrong, our clients come crawling back to their instructors with a million excuses as to why it didn't work out. Some of them used to the Old World way of skirting the rules and twisting reality to get what they want, and some of them simply determined to go on. Yet even the corrupt ones, apart from a few exceptions, are so crushed that instead of crawling back to their guard or section head, the most they can do is collapse into the arms of their loved ones. The clients' loved ones, who, after cheering the men on nonstop for hours, come running down from the balcony in the spectators' gallery with shattered expressions to comfort their husband, son, father-in-law, or nephew like a little boy in the few minutes of permitted contact before a guard comes on the PA and asks them to leave the hall. Soon after, the Institute parking lot is empty again and the clients who failed, having been through one of the biggest debacles in their lives, return to their dorms to start all over again from the beginning. Everyone has seen them fail, and any attempts to deny it are just a natural response to mental breakdown and moral collapse. There's no such thing as a mitigating circumstance. After months, even years, of intensive work with a client, to see them back in the classroom with men the patrol vans delivered only a few days earlier (or whose wives just dropped them off in the back seat of their sedan) is frustrating, we recognize. Yet the only "but," albeit non-mitigating, applies to the client's months or years of intensive work, which, as evidenced by their failure, apparently wasn't so intensive after all.

For us, of course, to some extent this is routine. The number of final exams that I've helped put together is in the dozens, and yet, despite having witnessed the miracle of new life so many times now, like a doctor in the delivery room, there's always something sacred about the suspense, and exam day for me is a day of great trepidation. The night before, I toss and turn just like my clients, running through their chances in my head before I go to sleep and again when I wake up.

There's an unspoken prestige that accrues to any guard who succeeds in bringing their charges into the New World on their first attempt.

A clean uniform is a must. It shows respect for both the clients and the occasion itself. I forgot only once, years ago, when my mother had been at the Institute on a visit and all morning long she'd been peppering me with maxims like "There's more to happiness than work, honey." The embarrassment I felt, standing onstage before hundreds of people, when I realized I was wearing a tracksuit dotted with cigarette burns (from my smoking buddy's wild gesturing over the fact that the Institute's director had accepted a post on some problematic European council that she felt "compromised the Movement"), could have been cut with a knife. I was thoroughly humiliated. Not only was my tracksuit burned, but it also had a greasy stain from an omelette my mother fried using Jaroslav's mushrooms.

With the gallery full, the hall where we hold the final exam has the atmosphere of a contemporary theater, but with the industrial beauty of a former meatpacking plant instead of a grandiose historical setting. It's normal now for artists to perform in these types of venues. The balconies, filled with the clients' wives, mothers, siblings, and cheerfully waving offspring, were created from the machine rooms of several elevators, which, ages ago, members of the Movement joined together into a single long corridor, offering a prime view over the entire hall.

I stand on the dais below, with the clients below me, scattered in bunches across the concrete floor. I gaze out over them with a feeling of joy.

Waiting for the exam to begin, the clients pace impatiently back and forth underneath the system of suspended hooks. Here and there in the crowd, someone points up and excitedly explains how the meat was moved from one place to another, which way the haunches went and where the broilers peeped their last just prior to their slaughter. Some clients go green in the face at the thought of the operation's scale, while the men clustered beneath the ramps alternate between debating about Old World nutrition and hypothesizing how the exam is likely to unfold.

People spent decades going back and forth about the problems of consuming meat, when in the end all they had to do was ban it: just like that, from one day to the next. Cancel the industry, slap the violators with fines, and look, no more ethical dilemmas (the companies were propped up with subsidies for a few more years, then the funds were redirected to other sectors of the economy while the employees all underwent retraining). Humanity breathed a sigh of relief.

It's an illustrative parallel, since today's test also reflects the straightforward logic that flows from simple premises. The proof of genius is in its simplicity, and once the masses are infected with an idea, they all start slapping themselves on the forehead that they didn't come up with it themselves, until one day they decide that it actually was their idea and they've been saying it for years, and that's the case for the clients pacing the hall here now, turning pale with anxiety. The New World was a conscious decision of their own choosing (it can be nudged forward by violence, but people have to set down the roots of thinking for themselves), the product of an immense and active effort, which the Movement only facilitated behind the scenes. An usher in a theater of processes that each person has to undergo for themselves, like learning to solve an equation with a single unknown. Though we largely keep this hidden at the Institute (frightened clients don't make progress), masking over the loneliness with the idea that their reeducation is taking place en masse, it's really not. They only live, sleep, study, and perform hygiene together. The client is a freelancer; the Institute, a program with user help preinstalled.

Sports have never really been my thing, but they offer all kinds of excellent parallels. Besides the "leap within a leap" from gymnastics, there's one other main one: with fair judges and no doping, cheating is impossible. Our instructors are fair (there's only one documented example of corruption in the history of the Institute), and, unlike the Olympics, we administer the doping ourselves, and gladly:

not only is rysol available, but electroshock helmets as well.

While I keep the mood up as master of ceremonies (after a brief introduction and some housekeeping, the clients strip down while I deliver a string of one-liners about sausages), women of all age groups and body types filter into the room like smoke puffed from a smoke machine, engaging the clusters of naked men in casual chitchat. The whole scene resembles a version of paradise multiplied, the Adams undressed, the Eves still clothed (awaiting my signal to strip), and this time no apple around to ruin it.

The men are at home in their bare skin by now, having tried it on many times before, while the women again are realies, actors hired off the street. In the event of a personnel shortage, we'll hire cooks, administrative staff, even guards to perform this duty, but only in extreme emergencies. Luckily, I haven't had to do that yet.

I take advantage of my privilege as MC to shout into the mic: "I'll buy a shot for anyone out there who can spot the director," and I say a shot because even if someone was dense enough to think we would invite top management to a gathering like this (they're holed up in the office as usual, but they generously gave me permission to make the joke), the alcohol reference alone would prove I was kidding, since everyone knows that booze is strictly forbidden till after the exam (the moment we let you out into the New World, you'll go and get plastered, it goes without saying).

And now I give the signal for the women to take off their clothes, and for any men who might be hiding behind the crushers (there are always a few shirkers) to come out and gather around them. Meanwhile the audience eggs the men on from the balconies. Some of the people who come to watch even spend the night before in their cars out in the parking lot, so they can be first in line in the morning to claim the best seats, since the Institute doesn't have enough rooms to accommodate visitors on that scale (another priority we want to work on), especially when you add in the fans of the Institute, who come even though they don't know anyone personally. They've been pushing us for a few years now to set up a refreshment stand, but we know the families aren't likely to consent to that. This isn't a movie theater, after all, but a place where human lives are made or broken, so, up to now at least, the director has refused.

The way the children horse around in the balconies it's a wonder they don't fall over the railing, squealing and shouting when they recognize their dads. Sometimes someone in the family will hush them, and sometimes I have to do it myself, though I try to avoid it, since it ruins the atmosphere, and atmosphere is crucial. On that front, cheering is helpful. It boosts the men's courage when family members yell out their names, and when the families notice that their men aren't doing well, running off out of sight to hide their erection, the families boo to show their disagreement and disgust. This happens to men primarily with the younger girls, which our clients haven't laid eyes on in months, sometimes years, apart from novices in tracksuits, who of course aren't naked. As the number of girls on the floor grows, there's increasingly no place left to hide, and although some men try to avoid the girls by hiding out in the corners of the hall, or behind the machines, it's an unsustainable strategy, since not only are all the corners already occupied, but the novices, tasked with monitoring the crowd, chase the men out of their hiding places and direct the realies, who are fewer in number than the men, to ensure that they're evenly distributed throughout the hall.

There are plenty of realies who treat the afternoon as an Old World retro party. For the rest, the motivation is money. It's normal for us to have a high proportion of realies from poor families. Still, to our delight, there are more and more women who turn down the offer from our recruiters, unwilling to play the role of an Old World woman no matter how well it pays.

Any men who get an erection are sent (sometimes by me, though more often by the novices who are down on the ground and so have a better view) to sit on one of the benches off to the side, so they don't disturb the others. They strode into the hall like kings, welcomed by standing ovations from the gallery, and now they've lost all hope. Collapsed on the bench, red-faced with embarrassment, they stare off dully into the middle distance, perhaps replaying in their mind that crucial moment when they still could have turned it around. Now it's too late. Their wives in the balcony hug their children, sobbing into their hands; the glow in their eyes has faded. Their offspring will remain fatherless for months to come (for understandable reasons, children tend to block this moment out of their minds for decades). Some of the women shake their fists at the men, fuming with rage. *Who'd want a loser like that at home anyway*, runs through their mind, and rarely, but every so often, they even threaten me. I of course pretend I don't see them. They're entitled to their anger, every bit. Only the client belongs to us—for the whole cycle, all the way through again, from the beginning. And if any of those women thinks it brings us joy, what they don't realize is what a financial burden it puts on the Institute and what a great disappointment it is for everyone involved in their partners' care. I look at the men sitting in anguish on the bench, and notice one, who clearly no longer gives a damn (which makes sense from a purely practical standpoint, but ethically just sinks him even deeper in the cesspool), beating off—as the crowning touch to his fiasco, I suppose.

I egg the realies on, yelling into the mic.

"Wiggle that ass!"

They seem to be losing steam.

"Arch that body like we told you to do."

"Spread those lips!"

"Right up close to the clients!"

And rub those breasts with the palms of your hands like they do in the porn from the old days, and all that other stuff.

I wave goodbye to a few more clients with hard-ons while addressing the ones still left (I always make sure to double-check all my equipment, but still end up with speaker burps and feedback from my mic), and the section head authorized me to weave some pop hits into the mix, so just for fun I throw in an Old World love song or two, and the realies' giggles fill the hall, and I also catch a few sly smiles on the clients strolling confidently through the crowd of women with their penises absolutely limp like it was an exhibition of nude oil paintings—and that's what we call the "New World ideal type."

For good measure, I toss in some references to Pavlov's drooling dogs, pointing out that we just condition our "subjects" with a different kind of dog food, and of course it's only a rough analogy, but in the context of that moment it's useful for the clients, since it isn't the kind of talk that promotes an erection, and if my section head were here, I'm sure she would suggest I go back to heavy breathing or those awful Old World tearjerkers.

I've been keeping track of MK, and he's doing great. Every now and then, he glances my way with a look in his eyes that seems to say, "See what a champ I am?" My guess is he can already picture being at home with his wife, since even a huge, shapely derriere and a pair of oversize breasts swinging in his face don't get the slightest rise out of him, and I'm even more gratified at the sight of OP, who seems to have intentionally worked his way into the midst of the youngest, chestiest crowd of women on the floor and isn't trying to avert his gaze even for a moment, the way I see some clients doing, though I let it go without comment (the novices on the floor serve not only to maintain oversight of erections, but also deliver messages from me to individuals), since I can see they're struggling bravely.

I can't help but feel a tremendous satisfaction. The months and years of work with my clients are paying off, and I also appreciate my work at the Institute because, unlike some operations, where you only take part in one small aspect of production (performing the same few tasks every day, inserting some component or other into computers when the robots go on strike) and end up alienated, I'm involved in the creation of new people from start to finish.

They came in as junk and we're sending them out into the New World as humans. I realize this thought is blasphemy and I can't say it out loud, but anyone who hasn't worked on themselves isn't so much a person as a half-finished product, and I wish all those women harboring silly prejudices toward men could be here with me right now, because humans are tremendously malleable, and the trick is to get their humanity on the right track and see it through to the end.

I'm more emotional now than I've been in years, and I order the models to step up the porn to the absolute max. A few couples are simulating lesbian sex, others are licking each other's vaginas, and even though we strictly forbid touching between the clients and the women, I see one proactive model groping a client's ass.

A novice who is standing nearby hands me a handkerchief, and it may be the mist of my tears, but even when one especially agile realie starts to tug on a client's member (I send the novice to ask her to stop), there isn't a single erect penis on the floor.

It's the first time in my life I've been in charge of a final exam, and not one single dick has spoiled it. I am present for the miracle of human transformation. With shaking fingers I switch off the mic and hand it down to another of the novices. The emotions I'm feeling now are not for public consumption. Not that I have anything to hide, but the clients should be focused on what's going on with their bodies and their revolutionary feelings, not wasting their time watching a guard go teary-eyed over her wards.

This is how the history of the modern age is written: in human bodies the Movement leads to reason and a better life. I close my eyes and picture Julie and Richard. They're in their new apartment, provided to them courtesy of the Movement for passing their final exams, and after a year's separation, they're anxious about spending their first night together. I can see the scene like it was painted on canvas, complete with New Age spiritual music. Man and woman undress, staring into each other's eyes, and the only thing capable of satiating their desire is the richness of their souls, the treasures of their two inner worlds. Their hands, caressing each other's faces, are heart readers, joining their bodies in conversation, and Julie's open thighs are the deepest invitation to dialogue there ever was.

I open my eyes, still standing there on the improvised platform, silence and emptiness all around me, including the gallery balconies.

Julie's letter to Richard has yet to arrive, but I know it will. True intuition has never betrayed me.

I tell the novices to leave me alone in the hall. There will be time to clear away the equipment tomorrow morning, before I take the clients on the field trip I promised to the torso factory. There are times when I just have to send everyone away and be alone with myself. For me, that's the most challenging part of my work at the Institute—the constant, everyday, intense contact with others. If the director promotes me to section head, not only will I get a raise, but I'll also have more time to spend alone in my office.

ALEX ZUCKER's translations include novels by J. R. Pick, Jáchym Topol, Magdaléna Platzová, Tomáš Zmeškal, Josef Jedlička, Heda Margolius Kovály, Patrik Ouředník, and Miloslava Holubová. He has also translated stories, plays, young adult and children's books, essays, subtitles, song lyrics, reportages, poems, and an opera. His translations of Petra Hůlová's *Three Plastic Rooms* and Jáchym Topol's *The Devil's Workshop* received Writing in Translation awards from English PEN, and he won the ALTA National Translation Award for Petra Hůlová's *All This Belongs to Me*. He lives and works in Brooklyn.

On the Design

As book design is an integral part of the reading experience, we would like to acknowledge the work of those who shaped the form in which the story is housed.

Tessa van der Waals (Netherlands) is responsible for the cover design, cover typography, and art direction of all World Editions books. She works in the internationally renowned tradition of Dutch Design. Her bright and powerful visual aesthetic maintains a harmony between image and typography and captures the unique atmosphere of each book. She works closely with internationally celebrated photographers, artists, and letter designers. Her work has frequently been awarded prizes for Best Dutch Book Design.

Always compelled by popular forms of storytelling—comics, movies, ads—Cédric Roulliat taught himself photography as a medium to convey his staged, artificial tales. The cover image of cloned men and women in a sterile, sunless environment might represent either the strictures of gender-conformist society or of gender-idealist reeducation camps—take your pick. The font used on the cover is CA Oskar by Cape Arkona, and is strictly separated from the picture to complete the boxy aesthetic.

The cover has been edited by lithographer Bert van der Horst of BFC Graphics (Netherlands).

Suzan Beijer (Netherlands) is responsible for the typography and careful interior book design of all World Editions titles.

The text on the inside covers and the press quotes are set in Circular, designed by Laurenz Brunner (Switzerland) and published by Swiss type foundry Lineto.

All World Editions books are set in the typeface Dolly, specifically designed for book typography. Dolly creates a warm page image perfect for an enjoyable reading experience. This typeface is designed by Underware, a European collective formed by Bas Jacobs (Netherlands), Akiem Helmling (Germany), and Sami Kortemäki (Finland). Underware are also the creators of the World Editions logo, which meets the design requirement that "a strong shape can always be drawn with a toe in the sand."